"Did you e

"Yes," Jean ans

"And still you think I'd reject you and our child," Josh said.

"Not reject. You're brilliant, and captivated by your work, not me. I don't even think you noticed how unhappy I was. You can't be that way with Jonah."

"It doesn't change that I had a right to know. You had no right to keep this from me."

"I accept that, but, Josh, am I really that far off? Do you know how many days you took off during the time I was with you? Three. You proposed to me on the front steps of your office building."

"We were sharing our success together."

"No. You were enjoying your success. I was just grafted in. Has it changed?"

"What do you mean?"

"Tell me, when's the last time you took a vacation? I chose to give Jonah the gift of not being ignored or sidelined by a long-distance man too busy to be a father. That's not a life for a child."

Allie Pleiter, an award-winning author and RITA® Award finalist, writes both fiction and nonfiction. Her passion for knitting shows up in many of her books and all over her life. Entirely too fond of French macarons and lemon meringue pie, Allie spends her days writing books and avoiding housework. Allie grew up in Connecticut, holds a BS in speech from Northwestern University and lives near Chicago, Illinois.

His Surprise Son

Allie Pleiter

HARLEQUIN® LOVE INSPIRED®

Recycling programs
for this product may
not exist in your area.

LOVE INSPIRED BOOKS

ISBN-13: 978-1-335-50955-0

His Surprise Son

www.Harlequin.com

Printed in U.S.A.

And be ye kind one to another,
tenderhearted, forgiving one another,
even as God for Christ's sake hath forgiven you.
—*Ephesians* 4:32

To courageous moms
of special needs children everywhere.

Acknowledgments

Special thanks to American Sign Language interpreter Kristine Orkin, NIC, DSPS, and to the friendly staff of Headwaters Outfitters Fly Fishing Adventures in Rosman, North Carolina. All of you were more than generous with your expertise. I hope I've done you proud and gotten the details of this story right.

Chapter One

Here comes the bride.

For Jean Matrim, the arrival of Matrimony Valley's first bride was a victory. She was looking at living, ready-to-walk-down-the-aisle proof that her long struggle to overhaul this town into a wedding destination was finally paying off.

Violet Thomas was going to be wowed if Jean had to call in every favor and spend every last ounce of energy to do it.

"You must be Violet," Jean said with her best everything-is-going-to-be-wonderful smile. "Welcome to Matrimony Valley."

North Carolina could be stunning in the spring, and the mountains were certainly showing off today. A clear sun dazzled through bright green leaves as they fluttered in the May breeze. The town was showing off, too. Front stoops sported potted plants. The sidewalks were swept, and many of the town's main-street businesses sported new coats of paint and cheery signage. Jean had even convinced nearly every shop on the newly renamed "Aisle Avenue" to put a little pot of violets in its window to welcome the valley's inaugural bride on her first visit. People had worked hard, and everything looked as charming as she'd hoped.

Violet certainly seemed to love it. "You must be Jean," she gushed, looking around at the small town and then up to the clear blue sky with its adornment of fluffy clouds. "Look at this place. It's just like I imagined." Violet beckoned to someone inside the car. "Come out here and look at it, Josh. It's perfect!"

Josh? Violet had listed her groom as navy captain Lyle Davis. She'd mentioned that Lyle wouldn't be on furlough until just days before the wedding. So this Josh—an uncle, brother or such—must be helping with the arrangements.

A tall, dark-haired man with intense eyes opened the driver's side door and stood up. At the sight of him, Jean was sure the Smoky Mountains behind her shifted a foot closer. The sight of this "Josh" pushed her so far off balance she nearly had to reach out and grab the car to stay steady.

Joshua Tyler stood in front of her. He still possessed the same powerful air of confidence she'd remembered, the same charisma that once drew her heart to his. Of all the people she never expected to set foot in Matrimony Valley, Josh topped the list.

Violet, oblivious to the shock wave going off in Jean's chest, and likewise in Josh's startled eyes, called him over. "Jean, this is my stepbrother, Josh. He isn't only paying for a lot of this, but he's giving me away at the ceremony. Right now, he's a great stand-in for Lyle. We've only got Josh for forty-eight hours before business sweeps him away again, but we can cover a mile of ground in that time, can't we?"

"A mile of ground," Jean repeated, still scrambling to get a grip on how her past and future had just collided right in the middle of Aisle Avenue. Her first bride was Josh Tyler's stepsister?

It can't be. There had been a time when she was to be Mrs. Joshua Tyler, but life had steered her far away from those days. Of all the hurdles she'd jumped to turn this town around and launch Matrimony Valley's destination wedding enterprise, a surprise like this certainly hadn't entered the picture in her mind. Jean wasn't even sure it entered the realm of possibility. Him? Here? Now?

Jean looked at Josh, searching for some hint as to how to handle what Violet clearly didn't know. Josh only stared at her as wide-eyed as she stared at him. One thing was certain: right now was not the time to get into the long and complicated history Matrimony Valley's mayor and chief wedding planner had with the man about to walk the town's first bride down the aisle. *Think, Jean. Be professional and keep this rolling. Deal with Josh later—keep your focus on Violet.*

"Let's start by checking in with Hailey," she managed. "You're staying at the Inn Love, aren't you?"

"Of course we are. Oh, look at the street signs, Josh," cooed Violet. "Aisle Avenue, Bouquet Lane—they've all got wedding names. Even the inn is called 'Hailey's Inn Love.' Inn Love, get it? Wonderful."

Josh was as handsome as the day she'd left him over five years ago. In fact, he'd aged phenomenally well, an assessment that sent up a poking finger of doubt into her not-so-phenomenally-aged stomach. She was fit, but she'd never fully regained the figure she had before Jonah was born. That never really bothered her until just this moment, when somehow Josh Tyler turned up looking even better than he had when they'd been together. The short span of years since they'd been engaged had fine-tuned his trademark confidence into the casual elegance of a sharp-dressed tycoon. Dashing, even. Seriously, was that fair?

Was any of this fair?

Lord, how could You do this? Today? To this wedding? To me?

Violet, bless her, still seemed oblivious as she pointed out the Aisle Avenue sign of the town's primary road that used to be Main Street. "You're already walking me down the aisle, Josh, get it?"

"On the Fourth of July, you can even parade down the Aisle," Jean explained, salvaging her professional voice despite the box of fireworks going off underneath her ribs. "We'll be doing that for the lieutenant governor's daughter later this year. A whole patriotic red, white and blue wedding."

Josh's command faltered for a moment, and he rubbed the back of his neck. With the jolt of shared history, she remembered he always did that when unnerved. Unnerving? Yes, that certainly described the situation. "Why don't I just grab some lunch while you two nail down the details?" he asked.

His voice. He'd always had a stunning voice—put to good use on the late-night shift of their college radio station. He'd stolen her heart with that voice, reading aloud to her under that huge pine tree on the west campus on warm summer nights. Back when the whole world spread before them. Back when she'd been a little lost and a lot reckless and…and now it had all come home to roost, as Dad would have said.

"Oh, no you don't." Violet's objection pulled Jean from the shell shock of her thoughts. "You promised me you'd stick around and help. No laptop, no conference calls while you pretend to sneak off to lunch. For the next two days, you're going to be my family, Josh Tyler, so get used to it."

Despite his smooth demeanor, Josh shot her a split-second "now what do we do?" look. They both needed a way out of this until they could catch their breaths and figure out what to do. "Your stepbrother does look hungry, but Hailey's dining room is closed right now." She looked at Josh, willing her expression to convey "helpful professional."

"Why don't you stop over at Watson's Diner for something if you like." She pointed to the diner storefront a block away. "Wanda makes a great BLT." She turned to Violet. "And there's no Wi-Fi to tempt him."

Violet laughed. "BLTs are his favorite. How'd you know?"

Not here, and not now. She shrugged. "I suppose you learn to be intuitive in this business."

"I thought you said we were the first wedding in Matrimony Valley. I love that. Lyle and I *are* the first, aren't we?"

"You most certainly are." The whole town would pull out every stop to make Violet Tyler the happiest bride in Matrimony Valley history. Jean *was* going to make this work, whether or not Josh Tyler had just cat-apulted himself back into her life.

Into *their* life.

Jonah. It really has all come home to roost.

Violet pulled on Josh's arm. "Look, Josh, that's the path to where the waterfall is. I told you the minute I saw it on the video, I couldn't imagine getting married anywhere else."

There had been nights back in school when Jean would spend hours describing her tiny hometown in the Smoky Mountains to Josh, including the stunning wa-terfall where she always wanted to get married. Sure, it had been Matrim's Valley back then, but how did Josh not figure out where he was going? Jean was glad Vi-olet didn't suggest they go look at the waterfall right now—she didn't think she could stand in front of that waterfall anywhere near Josh Tyler right now.

"Let's save that for tomorrow," Jean quickly di-verted. "Hailey's ready with your catering details and I've only got an hour before I…" She stumbled for a split second, not ready to bring up Jonah, or even say his name in front of Josh. "…have a family commit-ment, but Yvonne at the bakery will talk to you after we're done with Hailey."

She watched Josh's gaze flick to her left hand, and fought the urge to tuck the ringless hand into her pocket. His left hand bore no ring, either. So, a man she guessed to be one of Silicon Valley's most eligible bachelors also hadn't been snatched up yet. The fact lodged in her gut.

"I'll go grab that sandwich and meet you at the inn,"

Josh suggested, looking grateful for the out. "You want anything, Vi?"

"Wanda does an equally good tuna salad or grilled cheese," Jean offered.

"Tuna," Violet replied. "And then you get right back over here, Josh. If you're helping pay for things, then I want you helping me decide things."

Josh had never been destined for anything but success. Even during their time together in school and then out in California, he'd clearly been a rising star. But bright stars tended to obscure everything around them, and that shiny California life had grown complicated—and then soured—fast. How stunningly ironic that his business success now had a hand in funding hers, that her first big client came with her biggest regret in tow.

She watched Josh cross the street, feeling stunned and rattled. What on earth to do now? Dad had always called her The Queen of Solutions. But today, even Mayor Matrim, The Queen of Solutions, came up short. She hadn't the slightest idea how to solve her newest, biggest dilemma: how to introduce Joshua Tyler to the son he didn't know he had.

Jean Matrim.

Mayor Jean Matrim, and Violet's wedding planner to boot.

Sometimes life took a swing at you that you never saw coming.

The woman behind the lunch counter at Watson's Diner stared at Josh as if he were a science experiment, an oddity to be analyzed rather than a customer to be welcomed. As if asking for a BLT on wheat toast marked him as someone foreign and suspicious.

"We don't do turkey bacon, you know," she declared, even though he hadn't asked for it. "We only do *real* food."

"Big fan of real food myself," he said, offering a smile she did not return. The woman grunted what he hoped was approval, after which they stood in awkward silence as the cook started to make his sandwich. There was no one else in the quiet place, and Josh wondered if Wanda could hear the fierce growl of his stomach as the sound of bacon frying filled the air.

"How long has Jean Matrim been mayor of Matrimony Valley?" he asked. Jean would be turning thirty next year, same as he—how'd she get to be mayor at such a young age?

"Well, now, that depends if you count the year Miss Jean was mayor of *Matrim's* Valley. Before—" Wanda waved a dismissive hand "—all this business." Wanda clearly saw no point in hiding her lack of enthusiasm for the town's new identity, even to a customer. That might explain why Watson's Diner seemed to be the only local business without a wedding-themed name.

"Well, all totaled, then."

"Hasn't even been two years." Wanda drew herself up a bit. "My Wayne stepped in as mayor when her daddy first passed. Then she up and ran against him in the last election. Not too long after that she got the scheme in her head that turned us into…this other thing."

"You're not a fan of the whole Matrimony Valley campaign?"

"I'm a fan of staying in business, I give you that, but I can't help thinking there could be a dozen other ways to do it than turning ourselves into the Las Vegas of the Smoky Mountains."

Josh stifled a laugh at that. He'd been to half a dozen tech conventions in Vegas, and this valley was in no danger of giving that city a run for its money. "It's a pretty place," he offered, the urge to defend Jean rising up from some surprising long-ago part of him. "My stepsister Violet's thrilled to be your first bride."

Rather than offer a response, Wanda gave him a look that roughly translated to "I can just imagine" and hit the cash register key with a declarative finger. "Fries or chips?"

"Chips. And coffee. And everything to go, if you can."

"Of course." Wanda shouted, "To go, Wayne!" back to the cook, who barked "Okay" in return.

"Wayne and I, we're no big fans of 'to go,' but that's the way you young people all seem to eat these days. Next thing you know, *Her Honor* will be asking us to put in a drive-through window." She nodded toward a rack of chip bags on the wall behind her. "Regular or barbecue?"

"Barbecue, thanks." He probably shouldn't inquire, and he suspected her answer, but Josh couldn't stop himself from asking, "So do you think Mayor Matrim's idea will work? Matrimony Valley?"

"Well," she said after looking him up and down, "you're here."

I am indeed, Josh thought as he paid for his meal and accepted the white paper bag and foam coffee cup she handed him. *What are the odds of that?*

"I'm not knocking a single mother trying to make her way in the world, bless her heart," Wanda went on. "I just think we didn't have to turn ourselves inside out like this to survive. Matrim's Valley has been here for three generations and survived its share of hard times without changing the name of everything in sight."

Josh had taken two steps toward the door before he fully absorbed what she'd said: *single mother.*

Jean was a mother? She had said "family obligations," hadn't she?

It shouldn't have surprised him—Jean had always been the type to want marriage and a family. She'd worked in a bridal shop all through college. She'd given an eager "yes" to his proposal. They'd planned on a family, eventually, once the business stopped eating his every waking moment. Things never got that far. And now she was a mother.

But a *single* mother. A barrage of questions rose up in his mind as he crossed the street back toward the inn. For a guy who made his living on the internet, he'd been way out of touch with college friends. Did she marry? Whom? When? And what had happened to end it?

It should have been *him* she married. Of course, he had no right to say that now, but there had been a time when he felt that way. They'd been madly in love back in college. His senior year, he'd been king of the world, watching everything in his life line up to launch him toward the stars with Jean beside him. Nothing was beyond his reach. His final semester was a blur of parties and congratulations and that one spectacular night spent with Jean reveling in his golden future.

Things went too far after that night—and they both knew it—but they would have been making a new life together in San Jose, so it hadn't felt like a mistake. In truth, he'd thought that night marked the end of her second thoughts about joining him in California. He was so full of himself back then that he'd simply assumed he'd won her over.

She came to California, but she never really settled in. His relentless pace bothered her in ways it never had in school. She couldn't seem to make friends, claiming Silicon Valley's posturing grated on her down-home sensibilities. She grew so moody and distant that by the time news came of her father's illness, they'd both used it as an excuse for her to disappear back east "just until things got better."

They never did.

There were emails and phone calls, but the lapses grew longer as the flat-out scramble of a software start-up consumed his attention. He had always meant to call her but somehow never did. A part of him knew he'd have to face the wrong of that someday, he just didn't count on it being here and now.

He'd gradually shut down his connection to her, telling himself Jean was never really the kind of woman to take to West Coast life. It wasn't that he *couldn't* find her—he was a brilliant man with a fortune in technology at his disposal—he just never managed to follow through. He'd let her slip from his life, telling himself he didn't regret it.

Only he did regret it. And it felt like life was getting ready to show him how much.

Chapter Two

Josh paced his room while he waited for his chief of operations, Matt Palmer, to respond to his text. He'd asked, "Can you video chat right now?"

His eyes wandered over to the Welcome to Matrimony Valley brochure lying on the nightstand. Smart but simple, it had a folksy appeal that people looking for this sort of place would probably love. Right down to the cheery welcome from "Mayor Matrim."

A ding from his laptop announced Matt on the line, and Josh clicked open the video chat function to see Matt's face. "How's the brother-of-the-bride gig going?"

"Fine."

"Color scheme going according to plan and all that stuff?"

Josh tried not to groan. "I don't know. I think so. Violet's getting what she wanted, and that's what matters. She's the boss, I'm just the bankroll."

Matt made a face. "Aw. Will you do that for me?"

As Josh's second-in-command at SymphoCync, Matt

probably put in as many hours at the office as Josh. "I'll take that one-in-a-million shot, sure. I really called you to help me untangle a…complication out here."

Matt sat back in his chair. "What's up?"

"Jean lives here. As a matter of fact, she doesn't just live here, she's the mayor here. She's Vi's wedding planner. She's remade her hometown into this whole Matrimony Valley thing, and Violet's her first bride."

"Jean—wait, Jean your ex? Your ex-fiancée is mayor of Matrimony Valley? Whoa. Good thing this has no chance of getting awkward or anything."

Josh gave Matt a look. "I knew I could count on you to be helpful."

Matt shook his head. "Didn't she live in some place named after her family or whatever?"

"She did. If it had stayed Matrim's Valley, I might have seen this coming. As it was, it was all I could do to not trip over my own feet as we walked down Aisle Avenue in Matrimony Valley."

Matt kept laughing. "Aisle Avenue. Matrimony Valley. Seriously?" Matt wiped his hands down his face and attempted—rather unsuccessfully—to be serious. "So how's Violet taking this new wrinkle?"

Josh picked at the tassel fringe of one of the pillows in the mound around him. "She doesn't know. Jean and I…well, I think we hid our initial shock pretty well, and we're sort of pretending it's not there. She made like she didn't know me, and I did the same."

Matt gave Josh a dubious look. The man was a master of them. "You know that's not gonna work, don't you?"

"Of course I know that. But I don't want to mess this up for Violet, either. She'll get all weird about it, and believe me, she's high-strung enough already with the wedding. I've just got to get Jean alone to hash out how we're going to handle it."

Josh saw Matt pivot to another corner of his desk and begin typing. "Matt, would you mind finishing with me before you look up Jean Matrim online?"

Matt paused. "Hey, I'm just looking up where you are in case I need to airlift you out of there." After a second, he said, "Aw, look, there she is standing by the Welcome to Matrimony Valley sign." Josh heard more tapping and yelled at himself for not paying closer attention to Violet's plans before now. "She always was pretty," Matt commented. "Looks like she's held up better than you have. Little boy's cute, too, in an aw-shucks kind of way."

Josh picked up the brochure on the table beside him. The photo on it was just of Jean. "Little boy, huh? Someone told me she was a single mom, but I haven't seen a photo of her child."

"There's a photo of her with her son on one of the website pages. Third tab, lower left corner."

Josh swiped over from the video chat and pulled up MatrimonyValley.com, clicking through the website's pages until he landed on the picture of Jean with her hand on the shoulder of a boy.

He was expecting a toddler, but the boy looked older than that. Five or six, if he had to guess. He stared at the boy.

A boy about six years old. Josh stared harder.

A ball of icy lead landed in his stomach and stayed there.

"Matt, I gotta go."

* * *

Jean swallowed her exasperated sigh later that afternoon as she held the phone away from her ear. Her nerves were strung tight ever since the whopping surprise of Joshua Tyler's arrival. Josh Tyler, here, in front of her, in front of everybody. *Why, Lord? Why him? Now?* No matter how many times she prayed with her questions, answers failed to arrive.

Thankfully, picking up Jonah from school gave her an excuse for a quick exit not too long after Violet was handed off to Hailey at the inn. She counted it as pure grace that she was able to exit before Josh came back across the street from Watson's Diner.

Only being saved from Josh hadn't saved her from Wanda Watson. The woman must have been looking out her diner window waiting for the office light to turn back on, because the phone rang not three minutes after she got herself and Jonah settled back into her office.

"Wanda, you met him." Jean continued her attempts to appease the grumpy old woman. "He's a nice person. Violet is a nice person. Her groom will be just as nice when you meet him. You'll like the people who will come here to get married." That felt like an outrageous promise to make—Wanda didn't like lots of people. How did two sourpusses like Wanda and Wayne Watson ever manage a restaurant full of people all these years?

"I still don't see what brides and grooms can do for sandwiches and meat loaf," groused Wanda. "I don't care what you say, not every business in town will benefit from your little scheme."

It wasn't a scheme, and it wasn't little. "The man just

bought a sandwich from you, didn't he? Everybody's got to eat," she assured the woman. "The day before the wedding, the day after the wedding, the day they drive into town. Weddings and wedding guests mean business. For you as much as for Kelly's flower shop or Yvonne's bakery."

"You're banking an awful lot on this pipe dream, Your Honor." Wanda's *harrumph* practically spilled out of the phone receiver to douse Jean's resolve.

Your Honor. Wanda never meant it as a term of respect whenever she said it. Jean put her elbow on her desk and rested her head in her hands while Wanda went on about some other complaint—the woman seemed to have a never-ending list of them.

Jonah looked up from his coloring sheet across the desk from her, catching his mother's action and expression. "O-K?" The small fingers of his right hand formed the letters in sign language. His open hand moved toward his mouth, his thumb touching his chin in the sign for "Mom?" One little dark eyebrow furrowed in worried inquiry.

She smiled at him and made the sign for "fine" and "tired." Then, with what she hoped was a playful smile, she added the sign for "hungry."

"Me, too," Jonah's signs replied. His smile was as sweet as the grandfather he was named after. "Home soon?"

"I hope," she signed in return, grateful Wanda couldn't hear any of the conversation. "Our first bride is here for a visit, Wanda," she said into the phone. "Let's all welcome her the best we can." They'd had some version of this conversation nearly every week since last fall, when the town council approved Jean's proposal to change the town's name and become a wedding destination.

Was it extreme to change the name of the town, the streets and half the businesses? It was, but so was the rate at which the tiny town was suffocating under a dying economy. Tobacco was long gone, the mills had slowed and then closed, and nothing had ever replaced them. Something had to be done before there was no town at all. Weddings were what she loved, what she knew, so when the idea came to her she ran with it. Because that's what Matrims did.

Jean looked up at the portraits of her father and grandfather as Wanda droned on. *I did what I had to do to make everything work out, Grandpa.* Grandpa Jake had founded Matrim's Valley in the early 1900s, opening up the textile mill that transformed the loose collection of mountain tobacco farms into a bustling mill town. He even became Matrim's Valley's first mayor. "Built his mill and this town out of sheer grit and an unwillingness to ever admit defeat," Dad used to say of Grandpa Jake.

Her father, Jonah Matrim, had taken over the mill, and later the mayor's office, not long after her mother's death from an infection when Jean was in her teens. But even Matrim grit couldn't outrun a failing economy, and eventually the mill had closed the summer Jean graduated and moved to California with Josh. Dad tried mightily to keep the valley together, but it was as if something inside him that had started to die when Mom did continued to die with the mill. As if his own health depended on the town's. Her new residence clear across the country hadn't helped, either.

Josh proposed the day SymphoCync officially opened its offices that July, and for a while they were happy. Still, Silicon Valley's excess quickly began to taste sour in light of *her* beloved valley's demise. Dad had given his all as Matrim's Valley's mayor, and here she was, thousands of miles away, doing nothing she could count as important. Her dad loved her, doted on her, needed her, while in San Jose she was fortunate to get fifteen minutes of Josh's attention.

At first, Jean thought she was homesick. Or at least missing her dad. Dad and home called to her with a stronger and stronger voice until she finally went "for a good long visit."

She never returned to California, even when she discovered she was pregnant. The life inside her seemed to give Dad hope, helping him to improve. Dad loved Jonah in a way Jean had come to doubt Josh ever could. Especially when he was born, and maybe more so when they learned Jonah couldn't hear three months later. She never told Josh about his son, for reasons he'd now have to learn. Life was full of hard and painful choices. And even though such regrets drew her to finally discover the faith her father had, they still haunted her.

Failing health, like a failing economy, won out once more over Matrim grit. The pleasure Wanda's husband, Wayne, took in stepping in as acting mayor when Dad's health forced him to step down always bothered her. Still, with a toddler and an ailing father, it wasn't as if she could do anything but thank Wayne for his willingness to serve.

Except that Wayne's "service" had been a disaster. His single inept two-year term felt like one long stretch of everyone bickering while waiting around for things to get better. Someone needed to call a halt to the complaining and motivate people to do something. She was the last Matrim in Matrim's Valley. So when she dreamed up a solution—a drastic one, yes, but a solution—she bolstered up her courage and ran for mayor on a "Matrimony Valley" platform.

It took a while and lots of convincing, but eventually enough of the valley voted to support her. It seemed if she was willing to go so far as to swap out her family's name to give the valley a new chance at survival, everyone was willing to give it a try.

Well, *almost* everyone. "Did you hear me?" Wanda's sharp tone startled Jean out of her thoughts.

"I'm sorry, Jonah was asking for something."

Another snort of disapproval from Wanda. "A child playing in the mayor's office. Honestly. Wayne never did that sort of thing."

The "mayor's office" had been Wayne's idea, and consisted of a walled-off corner of the civic building that served as library, town hall, utility office and police station. *I will not be the Matrim who lets this valley die on my watch.* She would have liked to run the mayor's office out of the front room of the Matrim family home like Dad and Grandpa did—it certainly would make life as a single mother easier—but Wanda had talked the council into keeping the "improvements" Wayne had implemented. And in all honesty, this office was the safest place for Jonah to be next to his own home. Everyone here looked out for him.

Dredging up her last shred of diplomacy, Jean offered, "Thank you for taking such good care of Mr. Tyler. You know, Violet mentioned her groom was looking for somewhere to hold a casual get-together for his groomsmen before the wedding. Should I tell her yours would be the best place to feed a bunch of navy sailors?"

Wanda's tone softened. "I suppose I could manage that."

That was likely as close to cooperation as Wanda would ever get, so Jean chose to take it. She put a smile on her face and gave Jonah a "thumbs-up" sign. He grinned and gave her one right back.

Jonah. The joy of her life. She wanted him to have a valley to come home to, just as she had. He was the reason she fought to keep all this family heritage up and running.

As Jean ended her call with Wanda and packed up the beautiful felted wool bag she used as her "mayoral briefcase," she looked out the window. Tomorrow, she would deal with the tangle of Josh Tyler and how it might complicate the valley's first wedding. She would find a way through this, because even though this was no longer Matrim's Valley, she was still a Matrim.

So was Jonah. Taking her son's hand, Jean and her son blew a kiss to her father's and grandfather's portraits as she led him out of the office. *Lend me your strength*, she pleaded to the men who'd served before her. As she headed out into the evening air, Jean sent the same prayer up to her heavenly Father, as well.

It shouldn't have surprised her that Josh Tyler was standing in the middle of the street waiting for her. Patience had never been Josh's strong suit. He stared long and hard at Jonah. Josh's brain at full speed was an almost visible thing—his whole body nearly hummed with energy when his thoughts whirred into action. It had been one of the things that drew her to Josh, and it startled her that she could pick up on it so strongly after so many years had passed. It was as if her own heart could feel the chronological calculations going off like grenades in his head.

"Twenty-four Falls Lane," she said to him, pointing down the avenue. "The house with the green shutters. He goes to sleep at eight, so come by at nine."

"Jean..." he started to say, but she shook her head.

"No, not now." She turned as quickly as she could, heading Jonah toward home, feeling the rush of history as strongly as the fierce current of the falls.

Chapter Three

A soft knock came on her front door at 8:55 p.m.

She'd always known this day was coming. It had to come. Josh had a right to know he had a son, and Jonah had a right to know his father. She hadn't been strong enough to face up to the situation back then, and she was sorry for that. But she was a different person now, a stronger woman. The question was, was Josh a different man?

Lord, I sure hope You know what You're doing. I couldn't feel less ready to do this, but I'm going to trust You. Guide my words. Guard his response. He'll be angry. He has a right to be. But Josh is here, now, and I want to believe I'm strong enough to make this turn out okay for Jonah.

As she opened the door, his eyes told her immediately. He knew. Regret and remorse pushed down on her shoulders, a sudden weight that made her grieve over the choice she'd made back then to withhold word of Jonah from Josh.

Here we are. Stand, Jean. Stand and face it head-on.

She could almost hear her father's words from somewhere deep inside.

"Why don't you come inside, Josh."

He didn't move. "Is he?"

She hadn't expected him to blurt it out like that—as if the question hurled out of him beyond his control. Then again, she'd lived with the certainty for nearly six years, and he looked as if he'd lived with the possibility all of six minutes.

Jean pulled in a slow breath, gathering her strength and willing calm into her voice. "Come inside, Josh."

He came through the doorway, stopping to stare at a photo of Jonah she kept on the hall table. It was one of her favorite photos of her son, bobbing up with glee out of the water at the swimming hole, all wild hair and bright eyes. Josh stared at it, hard, his whole body on edge. He picked up the photo. "Is he? Mine?"

How many years had she pondered her response to the huge moment that question was asked? "Yes, Josh, he's ours."

He held the photo up toward her. "Ours? He's not ours, he's yours. How could you sit there and call him *ours* if you never even bothered to tell me?"

"It's complicated. Come into the kitchen and let's sit down."

He followed her into the kitchen, still clutching the photo. "I have a son. This boy…is…my son." He turned in a slow circle, raking his free hand through his hair before he sank into one of the chairs at her kitchen table. Not because she'd asked him to sit down, she felt, but because the power of the moment wouldn't allow him to stay standing.

"I've known I was going to have to tell you one day," she said as she took the chair opposite him. "I just planned on having a bit more time to figure out how to do it right."

"Right?" he snapped at her choice of words. "Doing it right would've been, how about—I don't know—six years ago."

"He is five. And I am sorry." She owed him that much. She owed him an explanation and an apology for what she'd done, even though she doubted he'd accept it at the moment. "California was a mistake. We were caught up in something that wasn't strong enough to last. We became different people once everything started for you out there." That seemed true for him, from her perspective. Had she changed as well without realizing it? Or had Dad's illness just realigned her priorities? "We weren't ready to be married to each other, and not at all ready to be parents. Not the way your life worked out there." *You were consumed with work*, she thought, but chose not to say.

"Are you kidding me? Everything was starting for *us*. You came out there with me. You said you'd marry me."

"I loved you. I loved who you were in school, back when all the success was bright and shiny. Once it became reality—the twenty-hour workdays, the crazy social circles—you had to know that wasn't ever really me, even back then. I knew I'd be alone. Married, but alone."

"That's not fair."

"Maybe not, but when Dad got sick…the Josh I knew in school would have been worried and cared and asked me about how I felt. That wasn't who you were when he got sick. You were too busy to care. I know you didn't mean to be that way, but you were. And once I found out I was pregnant while back here…" She sighed. "I knew it wouldn't work. You'd think you were capable of it all, of being there for everyone." She ventured a glance into his angry eyes. "But all I wanted was someone who would be there just for me."

"So sure of my faults, were you?" Josh's words were cold and sharp.

She put her hand to her forehead. *Give me better words, Lord. I can't botch this.* "Of course I wasn't sure. I wasn't sure of anything except that I was unhappy. Dad was… I don't know…sinking…and suddenly I had this baby to think of. Here you were, the son of this powerful judgmental father, and I was just this girl from a tiny town in the mountains. Then I got sick and Dad was getting worse, and…it seemed a better choice to stay here where I knew I had support than to be out there fighting for your attention."

That last part seemed to bristle through him. "*That's* what you think of me?"

Jean met his angry eyes. "Dad needed me here. You needed to be in California. I couldn't be in both places."

"So you decided how I'd react. And then you lied to me." He squinted his eyes shut. "This isn't how…this isn't the you I remember… Did I even know you at all?"

"I accept that I hurt you in this. But making a go of it alone with Dad felt easier than having to beg you for time and attention." She steeled herself to tell him all of it. "Or fight off your father's idea of what should be done."

She watched the words hit him, felt her spine stiffen as Josh stood up. "What do you mean, 'my father's idea of what should be done'?" The words were dark and dangerous.

She drew in a breath, willing the distance of the years to calm her words. "I don't know how he found out," she began.

He wasn't interested in preamble. "What did he do, Jean?" The words were sharper and louder this time.

"He came here a month after Jonah was born. He offered me a great deal of money never to contact you. I think he worried that if you ever found out, we'd be in your life." She'd never forget that afternoon when Bartholomew Tyler had shown up on her doorstep. The man was horrible. "He saw me—and Jonah—as beneath your potential. A liability best kept out of your life."

Josh put his hand to his forehead. "Of course he did. It's how Dad looked at everything."

"It made him furious that I wouldn't take the money, even though things were really tight then. But really, how could I live with myself if I had? He stomped out, swearing to find another way. A week later a very legal-looking document was delivered to our door, declaring I lacked the resources to properly care for someone like Jonah, and that he would sue for custody and have Jonah placed 'in a suitable boarding school' if I ever tried to let Jonah into your life." She shivered, remembering the disgust in Bartholomew Tyler's eyes—such a contrast to the loving way her own dad gazed at Jonah. "I think he wanted to make sure his faulty and illegitimate grandson was kept out of your shining future, and

if I wouldn't see to it, he would." She made no attempt
to keep the bitterness from her voice.

Josh drew both hands into fists and closed his eyes.
"My father has been gone eighteen months. He died
over a year ago. Why didn't you contact me then?"

"I didn't know he was gone."

"You could have known. You *would* have known,
if you'd just told me any of this. Five years, Jean. Five
whole years." Josh walked over and leaned up against
the kitchen counter. Her heart ached for him—this was
so much to take in all at once. Much of that had been
her doing; she was paying the price right now for not
telling him in all these five years, instead watching him
stagger under the blow of the things she'd just revealed.

"I'd like to say I'm surprised at my father," he said
with a sigh. "I'm shocked, but not surprised. It sounds
exactly like something old Barty would do."

The force that was Bartholomew Tyler was part of
what had made Josh the driven man he was, but it had
such a dark side, too. Josh had grown up believing he
was destined for greatness, but for his family, it was a
binding obligation, not a vote of confidence.

"Your father never approved of me, you knew that.
This just added fuel to the fire. We were welcome here,
whereas we'd have to fight tooth and nail there. I was
tired, still healing, and Dad was really starting to fail.
It was looking like it would be his last Christmas. I'm
not proud of how easy it was to throw up my hands in
surrender."

When Josh said nothing, she went on, determined
to say what she felt ought to be said. "Jonah is not a li-

ability. He's not faulty, and he's not an accident. He's a gift."

"A gift you hid from me."

"Parenthood doesn't work as a second priority. Jonah comes first in my world. He has to. Now, I suppose, you'll need to decide if he'll be anything more than on the fringes of yours."

There was a long, raw moment where they didn't look at each other. Josh walked back to the table and picked up the frame again.

"What's he like?" The single question seemed to pierce through all the pain in the room.

She felt herself smile. "Curious and smart, like you. Stubborn, like his grandfather. Opinionated, like his mother." She looked straight at him. "And deaf. Your son is deaf."

Deaf.

Josh felt the word push at him, like a typhoon trying to knock him over. He, a man who made his career in an electronic music application that was lauded for how perfectly it worked, had a son who couldn't hear.

The whole idea of Jonah's existence was such foreign territory, Josh could barely get his head around the fact that he had a son. His entire body felt still and cold. His lungs couldn't pull in enough air; his brain hurt from slamming together facts he had with possibilities he couldn't grasp. He had not just a son, but one with needs he couldn't begin to understand.

His thoughts whirled in a million directions as he tried to sort it all out. He stared at the photograph, somehow wanting the image to give him a foothold into the world he'd just entered.

It offered no grounding. As a matter of fact, it was a few moments before he realized he hadn't given Jean any kind of response.

"He's deaf." Not exactly genius dialogue, but he was working in shock mode here—eloquence was far beyond him.

"Yes. Since birth."

"So he can't hear anything at all?"

She was watching him, waiting for his reaction. Josh wanted to get it right, to say and do the right thing at this incredibly crucial moment. Still, the idea of a deaf son—disjointed speech, hearing aids, isolated from communication the rest of the world took for granted—was all so overwhelmingly new. Suddenly, being introduced to Jonah presented ten times the test it had been minutes ago.

How do I meet and get to know someone I can't even communicate with well? He wasn't even especially good with kids. The path to Jonah's silent world gaped like an impassable bridge.

Her eyes flashed just a bit at his hesitation, and he saw a glimpse of a mother's fierce protection. "He's not broken, Josh. He's perfect the way he is, just different." Her words and the jut of her chin dared him to try to pronounce otherwise. He didn't think of the boy as broken—at least he didn't think so—but he couldn't sort through the riot of thoughts going on in his head right now.

"Jonah is profoundly deaf," she went on. "Perhaps as a result of a high fever I had when I was pregnant—

we don't really know. When he wears his hearing aids, he can sense extremely loud noises, but not speech." She paused just a moment as if guessing his next question. "Or music."

He'd worked that out almost immediately, but the words had a stunning weight when he heard her speak them. *My son cannot hear music.* As ironies go, this one was huge and dramatic. Another realization hit him as hard as the first, and he stared deeply into her eyes. "Did you never tell me because you didn't think I could handle his disability?" Direct, maybe, but Josh felt he was entitled to be direct given the circumstances.

She paused before answering. "I didn't know he was deaf until he was three months old. It made things harder—especially when your father found out…"

"How did he know?" Josh started to shout, then remembered Jonah was upstairs asleep—then remembered Jonah was deaf—it was all tangling into knots inside his head. How was he supposed to act here? He didn't have a clue.

"I told you, I don't know how he found out. Does it really matter?"

"Yes," he shot back. "No. I don't know."

"It made it easier to come up with reasons not to tell you." When he shot her a look for that, she sighed and said, "You never had much patience for things that don't work the way they're supposed to."

"Things," he corrected, anger and betrayal churning in his gut. "Not people. I can't believe the way you think I'd…" He stared at her before sinking back into the chair. "Did you ever really love me?"

"Yes."

"And still you think I'd reject you and our child." It stabbed at him that she could think such a thing.

"Not reject." Her jaw worked, as if she was hunting for the right words. "You're brilliant, and when you're captivated by something, it's astounding. I felt astounded by you in school." She sighed. "But it was never about balance, Josh. I didn't truly realize that until SymphoCync. You were captivated by work, not me. I don't even think you noticed how unhappy I was. You can't be that way with Jonah. Jonah requires— deserves—lots of attention and patience. I didn't want to have to go begging for those things from you." Evidently, her talent for prickling his temper by hitting too close to the bone hadn't faded with the years.

"That's not fair," he retorted. But she wasn't wrong. He hated the fact, but she wasn't wrong. Silicon Valley, his valley, worshipped obsessive, workaholic people like him. Success out there demanded 150 percent of a man. He was just coming to recognize the cost of that—he was working on that with Violet now that she was the only family he had left—but he had a long way to go. "It doesn't change that I had a right to know. You had no right to keep this from me."

"I accept that, but Josh, am I really that far off? Do you know how many days you took off during the time I was out in California with you? Three. You proposed to me on the front steps of your office building."

He planted his hands on the table, rocking it a bit with the force of his gesture. "We were sharing our success together."

"No. You were enjoying *your* success. I was just grafted in. Has it changed?"

"What do you mean?"

"Tell me, when's the last time you took a vacation? How many nights this week did you sleep at the office? Violet's been telling me how hard it was to get you involved in this." She looked right into his eyes. "I chose to give Jonah the gift of not being ignored or sidelined by a long-distance man too busy to be a father. That's not a life for a child."

"I loved you, and you kept this from me. You never gave me a chance to keep loving you. You let my father win." The memory of what he felt for her rose up with a force just as strong as his freshly roused hate for his father.

"I believe you loved me," she said, her voice soft, "but I don't think you ever really knew what that meant. You thrilled me when you paid attention to me, Josh. But it was too rare. And I tried to tell you how unhappy I was, only you didn't hear it. You never really acknowledged how sick Dad was getting. It made me realize I could never really be the center of your attention. And then I couldn't risk that the baby wouldn't be the center of yours, either. Or become some pawn of your father's. So I chose what gave Jonah the best chance at happiness, and that's here in *our* valley."

Her accusations pulled at him like an undertow. "Were you ever going to tell Jonah? Or me? I mean, if I didn't show up here today, would he or I ever have known who we are to each other?"

Who we are to each other. The words landed heavy with significance.

"I meant to," she began. "Someday. I never set a

deadline or anything, but I knew Jonah would eventually grow up and ask questions. I think I was waiting until Jonah showed signs of wanting to know."

She rubbed her hands together. She'd always known this conversation would be hard, but in reality, it was excruciatingly painful. "That week, when one of your top engineers was out for a week with a sick child, do you remember what you said? You said families could be a distraction for a man bent on success."

"We were late for a deadline. I was frustrated."

"But even I could see it was how you felt. And really, isn't it the only kind of fathering you've known?" *Oh, Father,* she prayed, seeing his expression, *this is such a tangle. Only You can fix this for all of us.*

"But Jean—five years?"

She didn't have an answer for that, except to say, "Secrets get harder to reveal the longer they stay hidden. Dad always used to say we think they're staying hidden, but they are really just piling up damage, gathering weight and pain to release when they come to light." Gathering weight and pain. *Oh, Dad, how right you were. How right you always were.* "I wanted to be in a strong place when I told you. To be standing on my own two feet because I had no idea how you would react. I still don't. Do you want a family—a *real* family, Josh?"

"I don't know. I wouldn't classify what I had as a real family. I hardly remember Mom. I just know Dad and his weapons-grade wielding of expectations."

She couldn't argue with his assessment. Josh's father had been alone since Josh's mother died in a car accident when Josh was ten. He'd never remarried—until he met Violet's mother sometime in the past five years. Bartholomew Tyler was the furthest thing from what she knew a father to be, the furthest thing from the loving acceptance she'd known from Dad.

"I could have helped," Josh offered. "I *would* have helped. You had to know that. I can still help. I've got access to all kinds of technologies, adaptations…"

And there it was. Already. A glimpse of what she feared. "Helped?" she questioned. "Or tried to fix? This is exactly what I meant. You hurl solutions at a problem until it surrenders. That's who you are, what makes you successful, but that's not how to love a child like Jonah." She picked up the frame and held it toward him. "We know what technologies are out there. We see a specialist in Charlotte twice a year. But Jonah isn't a problem to solve, Josh. He's a boy to love."

"I get that."

"Do you? Do you really?"

She got up and picked up an old little wind-up truck that sat on the counter. "Roma Tompkins—she owns the antique store in town—she gave this to Jonah for his first birthday." She wound it up, and it made the wild buzzing that always made Jonah laugh. "It tickles his palms, and he laughs. His laugh is one of my favorite sounds in the world."

She set the toy down in front of Josh. "It's not slick or fancy or even new. But Jonah loves it. To you, it may look like Matrimony Valley may lack for a lot of things, but people here love us. For who we are. Can you do that?"

"I deserve the chance to try, don't you think?"

Do you deserve the chance to break my son's heart?

she thought. *I don't know yet.* "People here have learned sign language just so they can talk to Jonah. The church set up a class and all kinds of people came." Jean remembered being moved to tears at the standing-room-only sessions. She may be a single mother, but she was *never* alone here. She knew, even then, that she'd have been far more alone surrounded by strangers in San Jose.

"The kindergarten teacher here has a sister who is deaf, so she's fluent in sign language. He doesn't need a special class or an interpreter—do you know what a blessing that is?" she went on. "Jonah finds a way to talk to everyone, and everyone manages to find a way to talk to him. He's not lacking for anything, really."

"Except a father," Josh said, sounding as if someone had just pulled the rug out from underneath his perfectly engineered life. She supposed, in some way, that's exactly what she'd just done.

"Jonah has a father," she replied. "He's just never had a daddy. Are you ready to change that?"

Chapter Four

Josh stood next to his stepsister at the foot of "Matrimony Falls" the next morning. The site was as beautiful as Jean had described back on those starlit evenings lying on a blanket on the college lawn. As he stared at the sheets of water tumbling urgently down the endless staircase of stones, it was easy to see why she spoke of them with such awe. The gentle roar drowned out the whole world—not in the loud sense, but in the sense that it felt like a bastion of peace. Violet was right; there was something frozen in time about this place that made it an ideal setting to capture a milestone moment like getting married.

Still, the strange discord of being here with Jean Matrim, knowing what he knew now, challenged any real sense of peace. He'd barely slept after leaving Jean's home, and he doubted she fared much better from the circles under her blue eyes.

"We'll be the first to marry here?" Violet asked again.

"In a manner of speaking, yes," Jean replied. Josh

marveled at how she was able to play it so cool when he fought the dizzying sensation of his world turning in loopy, tangled circles, of his past colliding with his present while staring down his future. "I'm sure you can see why local brides and grooms have chosen Matrim's Falls for their ceremonies for years. You and Lyle, however, will be the first to tie the knot at the foot of Matrimony Falls."

Violet beamed and offered Josh the love-struck smile she'd been giving him with every such comment since they arrived. It was sweet, in a slightly obsessive way, how taken she was with the place and the idea of being Matrimony Falls' first official bride.

"You'll be the first to use this lovely new gazebo built just for weddings, too. And the first bride to walk down that flagstone aisle." She pointed to a path of carefully laid stones that wound its way between the two wooden platforms where he assumed the guest chairs would be placed. "God's very own chapel of leaves," she said.

Jean talked about her dad and grandpa spouting lines like that all the time. Neither Josh nor she had much time for spirituality back in school, and he still didn't, but the tone behind her words and their conversation last night told him priorities had shifted for Jean. Didn't everyone say becoming a parent did that to people?

One thing hadn't changed: she was as beautiful as he remembered. The long blond hair that entranced him back in school was cut to a sensible crop just off her shoulders. The crazy, dangly earrings she'd favored were now replaced by small gold knots. She didn't look old by any means, but she didn't look young, either.

Now a quiet grace filled her features. There had been a time when he felt he knew everything about her, but had he really? This morning it felt as if he knew next to nothing.

When would they get more time to talk about this? He was here for only forty-eight hours—and this felt like it would take weeks to untangle.

"It's stunning," Josh said, mostly for Violet's sake, but the scenery really was breathtaking. If all these wedding-ready amenities were Jean's doing, he was impressed. "You built all this up recently?"

"The whole town's pitched in to create what we've got now," Jean replied. "Rob Falston from the hardware store built the gazebo. Dave and Maureen Rodgers laid the flagstone aisle from stone their son gave them." She gestured toward the falls. "Of course, no one takes credit for the natural beauty and atmosphere of Matrimony Falls—that's God's doing." She leaned in. "But even God's green grass can stain a white dress and be tricky in heels, so we added the stones."

"See?" Violet smiled. "I told you Jean thinks of everything." His sister held up the swatches of fabric—the wedding party's colors—and the three lengths of ribbon the florist, Kelly, had given them yesterday. "See how it all works together, Josh?"

He could see that. He'd just grasped the full extent of it two meetings ago and had a whole lot of other things on his mind now. "Very pretty, Vi."

Jean gave him a look that told him he hadn't entirely hidden his level of distraction. "There are so many details to a wedding," she commiserated. "It can get a bit overwhelming. We hope to add another wedding planner at the end of the year so that we can keep up the individualized attention to each bride as we grow. But you, as our first, get my full attention."

Violet grinned even wider. Josh really was happy for her. They had only each other now, with the father they shared and both their mothers gone, so he wanted to help—logistically and financially. It was just that Jean and Jonah had completely blindsided him.

"Why don't you go stand at the top of the aisle, Violet, and take in the view," he suggested to his stepsister. "I always look out from the podium an hour before I give a big speech. It makes it feel familiar, and you'll be less nervous when you stand there on your wedding day."

"Great idea," said Violet, who handed Josh her notebook and turned to walk up the aisle to the trellis that marked the bride's entrance into the clearing.

When Violet was a dozen yards away, Josh took half a step closer to Jean. While still keeping his smiling gaze on his stepsister, he leaned in and said, "When can I see him?"

Her sigh was enormous. "I don't know."

"What do you mean you don't know? I'm his father. When can I see him?"

"Try to understand how difficult this is. You can't just show up in his life, Josh. We need to think about this, figure out how to introduce you in a way Jonah can understand and cope with. He's five years old. Most of this is way over his head."

Josh ran his hands through his hair. "I can't believe I'm having this conversation. I can't believe I have to

figure out a way to introduce myself to my own son."
He looked at her. "Have you said anything to Violet?"

"Of course not. Have you?"

"Are you kidding? I have no idea how to handle this.
Or what to say, if anything."

Violet came back down the aisle, then stood with one
hand on her hip, her gaze tacking back and forth between him and Jean. "Okay," she said slowly. "What's
going on here?"

Josh's first thought was *You'd have to be blind and
deaf not to see what's going on here*, but now that felt
like a terrible, tasteless thought to have. "Um… Vi, I…"

Jean took charge of the conversation. "The truth is,
Violet, that your brother and I have…a bit of a history."

Violet's eyes popped open wider. "What kind of
history?"

"In college. After. We were…together." *And the
award for colossal oversimplification goes to…*

"You and Mayor Jean?" Violet's eyes opened wider,
if that was possible. "Wait…wait, she's *that* Jean? Wow.
What are the odds?"

"I've been asking myself that for the past eighteen
hours," Josh replied.

"You know," Violet said, "I think I'll just head on
back to Kelly at the flower shop and go over these colors again. Or order more centerpieces. Leave you two
kids to settle things." Being three years older than Violet, Josh took issue with the "you two kids" remark,
but not enough to say anything.

"Do whatever makes you happy," he told his stepsister.

"Or takes a lot of time," she added, smirking. "Remember we've got lunch reservations to taste the entrées at eleven thirty." Violet looked at Jean. "You're welcome to join us, you know. I expect you could tell me a few great stories about my stepbrother here."

Her suggestion would take the awkward level off the charts, and Josh wondered if Violet didn't realize that, or simply didn't care.

"You're sweet to offer, Violet, but I'm sure Hailey can take perfect care of you."

"See you at lunch, then," Josh said with tightly forced cheer. Violet would have a long list of questions, surely none of which he knew how to answer quite yet.

"Bye." Violet took one last look at them as she started on the path that led back to town. "You. Two. In college. Wow."

Josh heard Jean push out a breath just as he released his own exhale once she was out of sight. "Wow indeed." He took a step toward Jean. "I mean it, though. We're only here until tomorrow afternoon. You've got to let me meet him."

Jean leaned against the gazebo. "I know it's a lot to ask, but I think it's best if he meets you without knowing who you are just yet. He needs time to adjust to the situation. I can barely handle it as it is, much less find the right way to explain it to him on short notice." She looked up at him. "Can you handle that? Meeting him first as Josh Tyler, brother of the bride, instead of Long-Lost Dad?"

Long-Lost Dad. Words Josh still couldn't believe applied to him. The list of ways he felt unready to be a father could fill a phone book at the moment. He ran his hand down his face. "Yeah, I suppose you're right. But how do I…speak to him? Or him to me?"

"The same way lots of people do—through me." She waved her hand in a silent "hello."

"And some things are universal. A smile, a wave, a handshake—" she brightened with a sudden idea "—or a milkshake. Why don't you meet us at Marvin's ice cream parlor at two thirty?"

"I can do that." He couldn't *not* do that—no way was he leaving Matrimony Valley without meeting Jonah, even if it had to be under forced and not-entirely-forthright circumstances.

"Do you want to tell Violet about Jonah?"

"No. Not yet. Not until I have my head around this. I'm hoping there's a way to not let the wedding get all weird because of this."

Jean gave a tense laugh. "I know this is hard. For both of us. But I'd like to think we can avoid messing this up for Violet. Or for anyone. Violet's wedding needs to be perfect for a lot of reasons bigger than you and me and Jonah."

"I get that."

Her eyes met his. "I can't believe I didn't put this together earlier. She'd mentioned a brother Josh more than once, and I saw your name on a form somewhere. I remember thinking, 'Isn't that a funny coincidence?' I never dreamed…"

"Me neither."

"I know what Dad would say." Her gaze cast back to the waterfall spilling behind them.

"What's that?"

"That there are no coincidences. Only ways God surprises us."

He hadn't set foot in a church since Dad's funeral—and it had felt cold and foreign that day, despite Violet's very friendly congregation. "Well," he replied, "count me surprised."

Jean held tight to Jonah's hand as they walked down the street. She squeezed his hand three times—their private signal for "I love you"—as they walked, and her heart pinched as her son gave three squeezes back. Her mind cast back to the final day Jonah came to visit Dad in the hospital, and how he kept squeezing his grandfather's hand three times. The moment Dad wasn't aware enough to squeeze in reply still ranked as one of the most heartbreaking moments in all of Dad's passing. Tears stung her eyes just thinking about it now.

She tugged gently on Jonah's hand to get his attention, then pointed to her friend Kelly Nelson's Love in Bloom Flower Shop.

"Stop and see Lulu's mom?" she signed to Jonah. She didn't really need to settle any floral details for Violet's wedding, but she needed to talk out what was happening with Kelly.

Jonah raised his eyebrows and made the sign for "cookie?" in reply.

Kelly often kept a stash of goodies for her daughter, Lulu, and Jonah to share at the shop. "Maybe one." She held up a single finger as she led Josh toward the door.

"Hello, you two!" Kelly said, setting a vase on the counter. "Good timing—I just put a fresh pot of coffee on." She looked down at Jonah, signing, "Lulu's at a friend's, but I still have cookies."

Jonah's head bobbed in a "yes" that needed no translation.

"Can we set out a few coloring pages with those, Kelly?" Jean asked. "I need to talk."

Kelly raised a questioning eyebrow. "Oh. I see." She waved Jean and Jonah toward her work area in the back of the shop. "Maybe I should get out my stash of chocolate croissants from the bakery? Has it been that kind of day already?" she called over her shoulder as she pulled out cookies, crayons and the stack of coloring books she always kept to keep customers' children occupied. "Our first bride looks pretty happy to me. And that brother of hers—quite the handsome fellow."

Everyone always noticed Josh. He effortlessly commanded a room back then, and it wasn't any different now. "No croissants. I'd eat a dozen. But I won't turn down coffee." Best to just spit it out while Jonah was occupied. Jean slipped onto one of a pair of stools after settling Jonah at the end of a smaller table. "It's actually the brother I need to talk about."

"The brother?" Kelly came back with two steaming cups of coffee and slipped onto the stool opposite Jean. "Isn't it usually brides who cause the trouble?"

The scent of Kelly's cinnamon coffee felt like just what she needed. Well, that and an hour's conversation. She'd be grateful for twenty minutes if Jonah didn't start getting antsy. "This problem isn't wedding related. Well, not directly."

Kelly took a sip of coffee while she sorted through some stems of luscious white roses. "Meaning?"

Just say it. You need someone else on the planet to know. With a quick glance to make sure Jonah's attention was on the cookies and crayons, she unnecessarily whispered, "That brother, Joshua Tyler, is Jonah's father."

Kelly nearly dropped the bouquet. "What?"

"Our bride's stepbrother is the man I was engaged to when I came back. He is Jonah's biological father."

Kelly scowled. "And he hasn't shown up before today?"

"That's because he hasn't known about Jonah until today. It's…complicated."

Kelly's gaze shifted between Jonah and Jean. "You mean to tell me that somehow Jonah's father showed up in Matrimony Valley as the brother of our first bride? Without knowing you were here?"

Kelly's sense of astonishment felt comforting. The situation really did merit the overwhelming shock Jean had been feeling since Joshua Tyler got out of that car yesterday.

Had it really been only yesterday?

"Sounds outrageous, doesn't it?"

"Unbelievable. Did you…tell him? Did he meet Jonah?"

"I told him. He worked it out before I told him. It's not a big reach for a brilliant engineer to count to five. And there is a resemblance."

At just that moment, Jonah looked up at her, and there it was—Josh in his eyes. It wasn't as if she hadn't seen it before, but it seemed to shout at her right now. "Juice?" he signed.

"Sure, sweetie," Kelly signed back, hopping up from

her stool to fetch a juice box from next to the buckets of flowers in the shop cooler. "How'd he take the news?" she asked.

"How anyone would take discovering they were a father after you'd hid it from him for five years." She'd hid it from everyone—well, everyone except Bartholomew Tyler and Dad—and the weight of that secret caught up with her now. She could no longer be sure it had been the right decision. Had she protected Jonah from rejection? Or deprived him of his father?

"So, not well." Kelly returned to her stool.

"I don't really know. He was more shocked than angry, I think. He's asked to meet Jonah. In thirty minutes, actually."

"Are you ready? Is he ready?"

Jean felt her face heat up with the threat of surprising tears. "Of course I'm not ready. I know Josh's surprise was ten times the size of mine, but I'm still reeling. I've thought about this since the day I learned I was pregnant. I thought I was preparing myself, but this is all too fast. I've decided Jonah will meet him as Violet's brother for now. It's not perfect, but I don't want Jonah's heart broken if Josh doesn't stay in his life. And I don't trust Josh to stay in his life—at least not yet." She let her head fall into her hands. "Why did this have to happen now?"

"You've maxed out your drama quotient, I'll give you that." Kelly leaned over the table, nodding toward Jonah. "So he doesn't know."

"No. I've told you a bit about what Josh was like when we were in California. I can't bring myself to set Jonah's hopes up for something he may not have in the end."

"I know things weren't good when you were out there, but could he have helped? Been involved? I mean, the guy's helping his sister get married. He's got to be a stand-up guy in some respects if he's here doing that."

"Stepsister," Jean corrected. "They don't have the same last name. That's why I never connected the dots on this."

"Well, sure. I mean, who would think? There have to be thousands of Josh Tylers in the world." Kelly cleaned leaves off the rose stems. "But he shows up here, now." She offered Jean a sympathetic smile. "You sure you don't want a croissant? I'd need three."

The tiny laugh that escaped Jean made this feel like the first lighthearted moment since this whole tense day began. "No. This and your sympathy are fine. And your discretion. I can't let this get out—at least not yet."

Kelly put a hand to her chest. "Cross my heart. Wow. I mean, really wow. It's crazy. But it could be crazy good, right?"

"Or crazy bad. Josh was a workaholic in the third degree then. I can't believe that's changed much. He lived life at a hundred miles an hour back when we were together, and I got left in the wake. I don't have any faith he can be a good influence on Jonah." She swirled her spoon in the rich brew. "I've got to be really careful." She considered telling Kelly about Bartholomew's cruel offer, but opted against it. Why complicate an already complicated situation with a dead man's cruelty that no longer mattered? "Most of the reasons I had for keeping this from Josh haven't changed. Only now I've got to find a way to live with the fact that he knows."

Kelly narrowed her eyes at Jean, wiggling the scissors in her hand. "You don't still… I mean…there's nothing *between* you two after all this time, is there?"

Jean put her coffee down with enough force to spill a bit, and Jonah looked up. "Absolutely not!"

"Okay," Kelly said. "Just asking. He looks rich and handsome."

Jean gave Kelly a look.

"…And he's a jerk. We don't like him or trust him. Got it."

"I don't *know* him, Kelly. I kept out of his life. I wasn't the kind of person who could stand up to him then. So I just shut down that part of my history."

"You didn't look him up on the internet now and then? Weren't curious who he turned out to be? I'd be cyberstalking the guy if I were you."

"Dad got sick, and my attention had to be here." That wasn't anywhere near a complete answer, and she was glad Kelly didn't press the point.

Jonah finished coloring one page and began leafing through the book to find another, humming to himself in the strange, off-key rhythm of his that Jean always found so fascinating. How did humming feel when you couldn't hear it?

I don't regret the way I brought him up. I don't regret my choice. I left because I knew what I might want would never stand up against Josh's big plans. But now that it's come back to face me like this, I'm filled with fears and doubts, Lord. I need way more wisdom than

I have. I need Dad, and he's not here. You can be my guide here, can't You, Lord?

"How are you letting them meet?" Kelly's question pulled Jean from her silent plea.

"Not as father and son, like I said. None of us are ready for that."

"So how do you do that?" Kelly asked.

"Milkshakes."

"Milkshakes?"

"Marvin's. At two thirty. It was the best I could do on a moment's notice."

"Well," replied Kelly, returning the now-full vase to the cooler. "It's as good a plan as any, I suppose. We'd better start praying now, and I don't intend to stop all afternoon."

Jean hugged Kelly. "Thanks. I'll need it."

Chapter Five

Marvin's Sweet Hearts Ice Cream Parlor looked frozen in time, as if Josh were on some midcentury movie set. Most of the "old-fashioned" ice cream parlors he'd seen were shops dolled up to look nostalgic. This *was* nostalgia—and not by design, but by definition: the drugstore soda fountain, right down to the black-and-white floors and the red vinyl counter stools.

"What'll it be?" asked the grandfather-aged guy in a white apron behind the counter, his scoop at the ready.

"Oh, give me a minute or two—I'm waiting for someone." He nodded toward Violet, who was out front on a park bench sharing her entrée decision with Lyle on the phone. He was grateful the groom had called; he needed a minute to collect himself before Jean and Jonah walked through the door. He was going to have to tell Vi at some point, but he couldn't bring himself to do it just yet, and the multiple levels of weird happening at this "innocent" meeting had him spinning like a hamster wheel. *I'm about to meet my son. But not as his father. And I don't know how to talk to him. I'm dying here, how do I do this?*

His own father gave him nothing to go on—their last few conversations had all been arguments, and he wasn't exactly swimming in happy father-and-son memories. Josh didn't know anything about being a father, except that he didn't want to be like *his* father. Jean had always talked lovingly about her dad. She had a model to work from, and it seemed Jonah had the advantage of a loving grandfather. *Don't muck that up,* his gut told him. *Try not to undo all the good Jonah's had.* Only…how?

Violet hung up with Lyle, a dreamy-eyed smile lighting her face as she pulled open the shop door. She looked around, the same "is this place for real?" wonder he'd felt upon entering visible in her expression. "Don't you love it?" she continued. "It's like some fifties movie."

The guy behind the counter chuckled. "I get that a lot." His face brightened. "Hey, you're our bride, aren't you?"

Violet beamed. "I am."

"Well, sugar, your shake's on the house, then. This the lucky groom?"

"No," said Josh and Violet at the same time.

"He's my brother," Violet explained. "My husband-to-be is in the navy, and he'll get leave just before the wedding. Until then, Josh is a stand-in and helper. We're meeting Mayor Jean and her son in a few minutes."

"Jonah," said the man, whose classic plastic name tag identified him as Marvin himself. "Sweet kid. I made sure 'which flavor' were the first words I learned to sign, you know?" Marvin demonstrated as he spoke. "Well, that and 'chocolate,' since I knew that'd be his answer."

I like chocolate, too, Josh mused. But so did lots of people—it wasn't genetic. The thought of someone carrying his genetic traits still sent him reeling.

Marvin spoke to Violet, demonstrating the signs again. "So, which flavor?"

"For me?"

"You're the bride. What flavor milkshake will make you a happy bride?" He pointed up at a sign that listed a dozen flavors.

Violet laughed. "Do you have a flavor that won't add to my waistline? I've got a wedding gown to fit into, you know."

"I can do any flavor in my special no-calorie formula," Marvin boasted with a wink. It was hokey, truly, but with a kind of down-home charm Josh couldn't help but like.

Violet planted her hands on her hips. "You're pulling my leg, Marvin."

Marvin spread his hands wide. "I am. Have one anyway."

As Violet and Marvin debated milkshake choices behind him, Josh looked out the window. A shock went through his chest as Jean and Jonah stepped out of the flower shop a few doors down and onto the street.

Jean. His mind cast back to another frozen moment in time, locked in his memory at age twenty-two. They were so *young*. The wind played with her blond hair and her eyes sparkled as she said "yes" to his proposal on the front steps of SymphoCync's brand-new office. She was still strikingly beautiful, but with the shades of harder years showing on her features. Her spunk had settled into a strength that struck him as a different kind of beauty. He'd loved the girl—well, as much as he could love anyone back then while he was scrambling to grab the world by the tail—and now he was staring, fascinated, at the woman.

What if? What if she'd stayed? What if he'd followed her here? What if she'd told him?

His brain raced down that maze of possibilities without his permission. It was a dangerous and unhelpful place to go; what-ifs served him in technology, but they could derail him in life. While Josh didn't know what he wanted from this encounter, he knew he didn't want to walk away from this with any kind of regret. This was going to be the start of his being in Jonah's life, not the end. He just had no idea how to make any of it happen.

And then there was Jonah. He bounced along the sidewalk like any five-year-old, hands going a mile a minute in what Josh figured must be little boy deaf chatter. Jonah must have said something funny, because Jean threw her head back and laughed.

Jean used to have this amazing laugh—a bells-and-wind-chime kind of laugh no one ever forgot. She still did, he guessed, although he couldn't hear from this distance. He used to go out of his way to do something silly just to make her burst out in giggles and feel the way it tingled in his chest. He watched Jean lean over and poke Jonah's nose the way parents do, all amusement and affection.

Josh couldn't muster up a single memory of his father doing that to him.

He stared hard at them, wildly ping-ponging between fascination and terror. *That's my son.* The words both pinned him to the ground and vaulted him to the skies. And took him everywhere in between. How on earth was he going to play this cool and casual, just an ice cream between friends?

And there was the whole complex issue, right there: *Could* he be friends with Jean Matrim? They'd once been far more, but those days were long gone, right? Now their relationship had to be defined by the grinning brown-eyed boy with the Tyler family wavy hair and long fingers who currently scampered for the shop door.

Violet was tapping him on the shoulder. "Hey, Josh, he's asking you what flavor you want?"

Josh couldn't take his eyes off Jonah as the boy peered through the glass door, grinning and waving his mother forward. "Huh?"

Violet ducked down into his vision. "What flavor milkshake do you want?" She overenunciated the words, as if Josh had momentarily forgotten English.

"Oh, uh, chocolate. Chocolate's fine." His heart was pounding. Josh had faced down multimillion-dollar negotiations and not been this unsettled.

As Jonah burst through the door, Josh caught Jean's eyes over the boy's head. Half a dozen things passed between them in a single second. Pride, nerves, questions, doubts, pain…he couldn't even begin to list the myriad of emotions zinging between them.

Thankfully, no one else seemed to notice. Violet told

Marvin to make a chocolate milkshake, while Jonah shot right past Josh. He turned to watch the boy scramble up on the counter stool behind him as Marvin said "Hiya, Jonah!" in a loud voice while his fingers waved in strange shapes. He assumed the signs also meant "Hi, Jonah," but how could he know?

How to do this? Sign language, he could learn. He'd picked up four different coding languages; sign would just be like adding another. But the being a dad thing? In this completely foreign context, with nothing to go on? He turned back to Jean, feeling as out of control as he could ever remember feeling. She just held his eyes, compassion and challenge warring in her expression.

"Marvin, show me that sign for 'hi,'" Violet was saying behind him.

Josh turned back to watch Marvin touch his extended hand to the side of his head and wave it forward, in a sort of vertical salute.

As if it were the easiest thing in the world, Violet turned to Josh, saying a cheerful "hi!" while she repeated the sign.

Jonah looked up at her curiously for a second, then signed "hi" back.

Violet looked at him. "C'mon, Josh, say hello."

Josh felt the heat of Jean's eyes from behind him. He took a deep breath, duplicated the sign and choked a bit on the words "Hi there."

I've just said hello to my son. I've spoken my first words to my son. His brain still felt like it was spinning.

"Two chocolate men. My kind of guys." Marvin's hands danced again in what Josh guessed to mean "chocolate" and got to work. "So that's a strawberry banana for the bride-to-be, two chocolates and, of course, mocha for Mayor Jean."

Mocha. The image sprung to life in his mind of Jean dumping chocolate milk into her coffee in college, of her ordering mocha after mocha at the corner coffee shop in San Jose. He used to know so much about her, but now he felt like he knew nothing at all.

Jean stepped over to the counter next to Jonah. "Jonah," she said as she signed, "these are my new friends, Miss Violet and..." She hesitated just a fraction of a second before she said, "Mr. Josh. Miss Violet is getting married here soon. I invited them to join us for milkshakes, okay?"

Jonah nodded, then slid off the stool to go sit at the four-seat table by the window. *He has no idea!* Josh's brain was shouting. He couldn't, at that moment, decide if it was better or worse that Jonah didn't know his identity. The whole thing was coming at him way too fast.

Jean reached into her purse and pulled out a pair of toy trucks, the kind that switch parts to become robots or whatever, and placed them on the table in front of Jonah. The boy's eyes lit up, and he immediately began working the intricate little pieces. Josh remembered that fascination with how things worked together. It was part of what made him so good at what he did, stringing together bits of code to do amazing things with data. *Is that me? Is that me showing up in him?* It seemed a ludicrous thought to have.

"He's adorable, Jean," Violet said as she and Josh sat down.

"Thank you," Jean said. She touched Jonah's shoulder to get him to look up from the trucks. "Miss Violet says she thinks you're cute."

Jonah made the face any five-year-old boy would make to such a gushy comment, but tilted one hand, palm up, away from his chin and went back to his trucks.

"That's 'thank you,'" Jean said. "Someday when he's a teenager, I'll be thankful sarcasm doesn't quite translate in sign."

"Oh, the things I said to my mother," Violet commiserated. She looked at Josh. "I suspect you were worse. Your dad told me a few stories."

Oh, you have no idea, Josh thought, a bit envious of Violet's cheer. Things always seemed so simple to her, so easy, and right now his entire life felt complicated and impossible.

Jean sipped her milkshake, the treat feeling cold and choking instead of tasting like the creamy delight it usually was. This was so much harder than she'd thought it would be. She'd thought having Violet and Jonah here and unaware of the enormous nature of the moment would tamp down the awkwardness. Instead, it had done just the opposite; every second felt heavy and as though they were dangling impossibly off balance.

Violet, cheerful as ever, suddenly stood up. "Hey, Marvin, will you indulge this bride with one last dollop of whipped cream before she diets like crazy to fit into her wedding dress?"

"I think every bride ought to get double whipped cream," Marvin said, brandishing the can as Violet walked toward the counter.

Jonah seized the clear path between him and Josh to scoot one of his little trucks across the table to bump right into Josh's milkshake. One of the little front sections snapped off at the contact. They came apart all the time—they were designed to disassemble, and that's what Jonah seemed to like best about them.

Her stomach tightened a bit as Josh picked up the small piece and the truck, examining them. He looked at Jonah, one eyebrow raised, but Jonah simply returned the stare. She watched the two of them, each with a truck, looking so much like mirror images that she felt a bit dizzy. Somewhere in the distance Violet was chatting with Marvin, but the whole world faded out of focus while she watched Jonah and Josh encounter each other. Father and son. Her son and his father. She'd imagined this moment a dozen different ways, but none of them ever looked or felt like this.

Josh squinted at the truck, turned it over a time or two, and then replaced the piece in an entirely new way. Jonah's eyes grew wide for a moment, and then Jean watched her son pull off a similar piece on the truck he was holding and reattach it in the way Josh had done.

Josh's face showed the same stunned awe she felt herself at this first "conversation" between father and son. How could a moment feel so small and so huge at the same time?

With a rather overwhelmed grin, Josh sent the truck scooting back over the table to Jonah. Instead of doing the same, Jonah picked up both trucks and matter-of-factly slid over into the empty chair Violet had left. The moment Josh looked up at her with his son sitting next to him, Jean felt such a bittersweet tangle of joy and regret that breathing felt impossible. Had she done the right thing in keeping them apart? Or had it been a huge mistake?

Jonah placed a truck in front of Josh and poked his arm in an unspoken "your turn." She watched the moment of contact flash through Josh, pulling in his breath and widening his startled eyes. After a wonder-struck moment, Josh set to rebuilding the truck pieces in a zany way that made Jonah laugh.

Jean was so mesmerized, she hadn't even noticed Violet sitting back down next to her in the seat Jonah had occupied. "Boys and their toys. I know that look. Lyle and his buddies get like that when they have the hood of his car open." She laughed and stirred her milkshake. "The universal male language of 'let's build something and take it apart again,' huh? No words needed."

"I suppose," Jean replied softly, feeling as if she'd tumble off the stool if she moved an inch. Violet, of course, had no way of knowing she was watching a life-changing moment transpire. Matrimony Valley's first bride was just watching a cute moment between a man and a boy.

Matrimony Valley's mayor, on the other hand, was watching her son meet his father. And watching the man she'd loved and left—or who had left her; it was difficult to know which was which anymore—connect with the son he'd never known. Within the space of a minute, the two had become totally absorbed in the mutual construction of tiny plastic trucks, trying and trading pieces in silent but animated conversation.

"I want a bunch of kids someday." Violet sighed. "Lyle does, too. Being an only child is a hard thing.

Was for me, and I know it was for Josh. Lyle comes from a big family, and I just love all that noise." Her face reddened. "Was that a crass thing to say, seeing as…?" She waved one hand awkwardly in the vicinity of her ear.

People often did that—feel odd about describing sounds if Jonah was nearby. "It's fine, really. I'm an only child myself, but I get what you mean. Sometimes it's nice to feel surrounded." Jean thought about the townspeople who'd surrounded her in the first days after Dad died. She thought she'd been used to silence, but it threatened to drown her right after Dad passed. There were too many nights where the only sound was the sobs of her grief, and she'd tried to feel blessed that she could cry as loud as she wanted in the middle of the night without fear of waking Jonah.

"Is it hard, raising him by yourself?"

The question drew a pointed look from Josh, totally misinterpreted by Violet. "What? Women talk about deeper subjects than this year's make and model. I think Jean's pretty amazing for what she's done, don't you?"

Poor Violet. She had no way of knowing she was happily skipping through an emotional minefield of history and secrets. Josh was going to have to tell her, and soon. They'd never make it through the wedding at this rate.

"Amazing," Josh said, looking rather lost.

Violet mistook his stumbling reply for disinterest. "I can't wait for him to wake up to the rest of the world outside his office door," she remarked, nodding with amused annoyance at her stepbrother. "Josh has been too much 'all work and no play.' He says he's trying to change, but as I expect you learned, once you wave an engineering problem under his nose he's lost."

Violet chatted away, and Jean tried hard to follow the conversation while watching Josh interact with Jonah. Once the milkshakes were done, however, and the trucks had been reassembled half a dozen times, Jonah began to grow bored and squirmy. She tried to be grateful he'd lasted as long as he had, but when a toy dropped on the floor and he bumped his head as he picked it up, peace was lost.

"We'd better get home," Jean said above Jonah's wailing. "This has been fun." It seemed like such a banal way to describe such a monumental meeting.

"Yeah," Josh said, looking equally lost. Would this be the last time they met? Of course not—he'd be back in a matter of weeks for the wedding. But what about after that?

She didn't know. She *couldn't* know, at least not yet. All she could know was that protecting Jonah from hurt had to be her top priority. But how? *I'm trusting You'll show me how, Lord*, she prayed as she gathered the trucks and headed for home. *Because I have no clue.*

Chapter Six

Violet stared at him as they ate the breakfast Josh had ordered up to his room Saturday morning. Her mouth hung open in shock. And she had every right to look shocked, given the bombshell of information he'd just dropped on her. "So, that's why I'm not coming back with you tomorrow. Not just yet. I need to figure out what to do here, and I don't think I should do that from California."

She planted one hand on her hip. "Well, that's good, because I think I would call up and cancel your flight reservation myself, considering what you just told me." She peered out his window in the direction of the ice cream shop where they'd been yesterday afternoon. "He's yours? Truly? I can't get my mind around that, Josh."

Josh ran a hand through his hair as he came up beside her at the window. "Believe me, I can barely get my own mind around it." He looked at his stepsister, feeling more unsteady than he could ever remember. "What do I do here?"

Her eyes softened, and Violet touched his elbow. "*What* you do, genius, is be a dad. It's the *how* that gets tricky, I suppose."

"You're telling me."

"You're there, he's here. And she's here. And then there's the two of you. I mean, there's history, and then there's this. It's a whole lot more complicated than just her being your ex, you know?" She grabbed his hands. "You have a son, Josh. A five-year-old son."

"I know." Josh squinted his eyes shut for a moment, the words hitting him all over again. Would it ever stop feeling like someone had just dumped him down in the middle of a tornado?

Her eyes teared up a bit. "It's a gift, Josh. You see that, don't you?"

A part of him could see that. Snapping those pieces together, watching the puzzle-solving spark in Jonah's eyes that was such an essential part of his own world, he could see the gift. "Yeah, but it's so incredibly complicated. I'm still sort of blindsided, you know? I feel like I need a million years to figure it out, but I feel like I have to figure it out right now. We're at a crucial juncture with SymphoCync. The timing couldn't be worse."

Violet smiled. "Finally a puzzle the great Josh Tyler can't solve right away. Or on his timetable. Would it be mean to say this is going to be fun to watch?"

He shot her a dark look. "Yes, it would. This is going to be a lot of things, but I don't think 'fun' is going to be one of them."

Violet crossed her arms over her chest. "Are you so sure? I get that I haven't known you your whole life, but I'm not sure you've ever learned how to do 'fun.' Seems to me a five-year-old boy could be a great teacher of that."

"Hey, my staff thinks I'm fun."

She tilted her head to one side. "Even *you* should know that doesn't count."

"So you're okay if I stay?"

"I'm twenty-six. I know how to get on a plane and go back to Nevada by myself. I did make it most of those years without your invaluable input, you know." She put a hand on his shoulder. "For what it's worth, I think you're making the right choice. Some things are more important than SymphoCync, even at this—" she made air quotes with her fingers "—crucial juncture."

Josh merely grunted in reply, not caring for the way Violet threw one of his favorite phrases back at him. But it did fit—this was feeling like an epic crucial juncture, for ways he couldn't even put a finger on yet. All he knew was a deep, throbbing insistence that he couldn't get this wrong. That all kinds of things were at stake, even if he didn't know yet what all those things were.

"Have you told Jean and Jonah you're staying yet?"

Josh looked back down Aisle Avenue toward Jean's office. "No, that's next. And then, I suppose, we figure out how to tell Jonah that...who I am." It was like the word *father* couldn't fit on his tongue yet. The title had all kinds of weighty baggage hanging off it that he couldn't shoulder. He didn't like the idea of anyone ever thinking of him in the sour, resentful ways he thought of his own father, and it felt completely beyond him to know how to prevent that. Every scientist knew the hardest thing was to prove a negative—how could he prove to himself that he didn't have to be the kind of father his own dad had been?

"I like her, you know," Violet said. "I'm impressed with what she's trying to do here, and I like being a part of it. Maybe you can help her out a bit while you're here dealing with the other stuff. This place is like a giant wedding program, only with people and places instead of users and data. They'll have a lot of bugs to solve. Could be a nice change for a guy like you."

That made him laugh. "Me? 'Debugging' Matrimony Valley? I'm not who anyone would want as a wedding planner."

"No, but you are a systems creator. And a problem solver. And very close—" she pointed to her chest "—to the person who would like Matrimony Valley's first wedding to come off as a spectacular success. That makes you a...what do you always call it? A high-value stakeholder."

Josh handed Violet the rental car keys. "You definitely need to go back to Nevada now."

"How long will you stay?"

He rubbed the back of his neck. "A day at least, maybe more. I can't stay long, but I'm not leaving until...well, I don't know what that is yet."

"Human beings are so much messier than machines, aren't they?" She gave him a hug. "Call me tonight—and every night you're here—and tell me how it goes. I'm pulling for you. 'Cause that's what sisters do."

This trip was supposed to result in less stress. It was supposed to nail down all the details for Violet's wedding so he could focus his attention on key upcoming events at SymphoCync. Now he felt like problems and complications were exploding around every corner. "I will." A small curl of anxiety wound up his back. Everybody in this little town seemed to love Violet instantly, but he didn't know how to connect with any of these people. He didn't even know how to talk on the most basic level with Jonah. There were no manuals, procedures or programming tactics to fall back on here—he was in uncharted waters.

Violet must have seen it on his face. "Hey," she said softly, "you'll be okay. You'll figure this out. You always do."

Somehow his technical prowess felt like no use at all in the problems ahead of him. "This is different."

She kissed him on the cheek. "Not really. Just use this part—" she laid a hand on his chest "—more than this part—" she moved her hand up to poke at his forehead "—and you'll be okay."

Josh wanted to believe that, but the faith wasn't coming easily at the moment. While he knew she wouldn't, a panicked, irrational part of him feared that Jean would tell him he couldn't stay. That he couldn't get to know his son and be part of his life. She'd made it clear that she left because she'd felt him incapable of offering her any real support. Looking back, he was coming to see just how much he'd taken her for granted. How he'd given her reason to think he wasn't ready for the commitment of marriage and especially family. She had no real reason to suddenly welcome him into her life. Not now, when she had no evidence that he'd changed and she was already facing the huge challenge of launching Matrimony Valley.

Violet opened the hotel room door. "I'll expect an

update by the time I reach Asheville and get on my plane."

"Since when did you start ordering me around?"

She simply grinned. "Lots of things have changed this weekend, haven't they?"

As Josh watched her head down the hall to her own room, he felt like *lots* wasn't nearly a big enough word for all that had tilted in his life lately. He finished his bagel, grabbed his phone and set off for Jean's house.

Jean stared at her email inbox as Jonah watched Saturday morning cartoons. She tried to work up the enthusiasm necessary to convince an interested bride that Matrimony Valley could deliver on a lovely wedding. Instead, she felt as if she could barely deliver a coherent sentence. Her thoughts and emotions felt as if they'd been swirling like the pool at the bottom of Matrimony Falls lately. Seeing Jonah and Josh together at Marvin's yesterday had pulled the rug out from under her in more ways than she could count.

Logistically, her son and his father were total strangers—but they weren't. They'd already connected, even over something as small as his "puzzle trucks." Josh had always been most alive, most vibrant—and most charismatic—when solving a puzzle or problem. There had always been moments when Jonah would look at her or crack a sly smile in ways that reminded her strongly of Josh. But seeing them together at Marvin's, both tinkering with those trucks, trading pieces and connecting without words, had made her question everything. It forced her to ask the frightening question: Keeping them apart had felt easier, but had it been right?

Had the cost of that separation been too high? Could any of that damage be repaired? *Lord, I have to believe You brought Josh here, now, for a reason. I'm just scared how all this will turn out. My brain knows I can trust it will turn out well, but the rest of me feels tied up in knots. He'll be leaving this afternoon, and I don't know how we move forward from here.*

Jean looked out her kitchen window, craning her neck to see if she could catch a glimpse of Josh and Violet's rental car in the lot beside Hailey's Inn Love. She couldn't see the blue sedan, and for an awful moment she wondered if the pair had left without saying goodbye. He wouldn't do that, would he? She didn't think so, yet who could predict how anyone would react in the wild situation they found themselves in?

Her eye then caught his figure walking across the street toward her. Without Violet. Even after so many years, she recognized the changed set of his shoulders—Josh's whole body seemed to change when he hit on a solution or even just a course of action. The man leaned into life in ways she'd never seen in anyone else; it was part of what made him an unstoppable force—for both good and bad.

She felt her pulse pound as Josh caught her eye for a split second before walking up her front steps. Even the way he knocked on the door was a declaration. He'd chosen a course of action, and she had no idea what it was or if she'd have any say in it—and wasn't that exactly how things had gone wrong in the first place?

Josh walked straight into her hallway. "I'm staying

another few days. I'm not sure how many, but I want to get to know Jonah. I want to figure out how to do this."

Jean's heart tumbled in a dozen different directions. "I want *us* to figure out how to do this, too." She emphasized the *us*, fighting a wave of doubt. Too many shadows of Bartholomew's ultimatums flashed in Josh's eyes.

Her reaction must have shown, for she watched him back off and soften a bit, running a hand through his hair. "Yes, us. I meant us. I'm...well, I'm not sure how good I'm going to be at this. Ever."

The warm smile she felt creeping across her face surprised even her. "Welcome to parenthood. It's just one giant doubt after another. And they tell me that's true under ordinary circumstances."

Josh rolled his eyes. "And these circumstances are anything but ordinary."

"Come in and have some coffee." As she pulled a cup out of the cupboard, she had to ask, "Can you afford to be away from SymphoCync that long?" The answer would tell her a lot, wouldn't it?

He shrugged as he leaned against the counter. "Actually, no. It'll make an epic mess of things."

And yet he was choosing to stay. Something the old Josh would never have done. It was an undertow of a revelation, shifting the ground under her feet. His staying would create an epic mess of things on her end, as well.

"Things are already an epic mess, wouldn't you say?" She didn't have to specify that it wasn't work related; they both knew what she meant.

He cast his glance toward the den, where Jonah sat. "I want him to know who I am, Jean."

The statement, and the insistent way he said it, set off a little cascade of relief in her stomach. She'd never really believed Josh would deny his son, but dismissal had always loomed as a fear for her. She'd do anything to spare Jonah his father's inattention. Now, for the first time, Jean let herself believe she might not have to worry about that. Josh wouldn't ignore him. He'd struggle, try and probably make a dozen mistakes—goodness, hadn't she?—but he wouldn't ignore Jonah. She could finally believe that.

"I want him to know who you are, too." The words caught with surprising thickness in her throat. "I'm just not sure how to go about it. Somehow I don't think, 'Hey, Jonah-boy, this is your dad,' is the way to go."

"I want to be the one who tells him." There it was again, the Tyler brand of determination—she had to remind herself it wasn't meant to feel so oppressive this time. "I want to talk to him. Learn whatever it is I need to in order to do that. I learned advanced coding in three weeks, I'll learn—" he waved his fingers in a bumbling approximation of sign language "—this faster."

But the "I'm your daddy" conversation was one that would require more than fumbling skills in sign language. Or would it? Somehow this felt like both the most complex issue in the world and the simplest. Still, a few more of the knots in her heart loosened at his determination to enter Jonah's world.

"So...is it okay with you if I stay on a bit?"

Jean had to swallow her astonishment. The determined force who had walked into her house a minute ago did not look like the kind of man to ask permission. The Josh she'd known rarely asked permission for anything—he hadn't even asked Dad for his blessing to propose to her, even though Josh knew Dad would expect something like that. With a start, she realized that while Josh didn't know Jonah, she no longer knew Josh.

"Yes, it is," she agreed.

"I'm glad."

An awkward silence filled the room, as if neither of them knew quite what ought to come next.

Evidently, Josh had given this some thought, for he reached into his hip pocket and pulled out what looked like a small black leather envelope. She realized it was some kind of fancy holder for a stack of index cards and a sleek silver pen. It was a flashback to the old Josh, who always walked around with similar supplies in his back pocket, ready to jot down whatever new burst of genius appeared. Back then the stack was usually a crumpled collection; now it was an executive-looking accessory—and was surprisingly "old-school" for a man who made his living in the digital world.

"Yeah," he said, following her gaze. "I still do this."

"No cyber-dictated notes downloaded to the cloud or whatever?"

He gave a boyish grin. "Uploaded. Yes, I do those, too. But I never quite could kick this habit." He pulled a card from the holder, and she noticed they were not the kind of index cards you could get at the five-and-dime down the street. These were a rich sky blue color and engraved with his initials, *JBT*, in one corner. She couldn't see the words, but could see it was a list. "I've put together some questions," he said, clicking the silver pen.

"Okay." She set the coffee down on the table, and they sat down.

"What's Jonah's favorite food?"

She was expecting questions about their history, Jonah's condition, what she'd been doing the past few years. His inquiry was a pleasant surprise. "Fish sticks. With ketchup, not tartar sauce."

He gave an expected grimace. She could barely stomach how Jonah doused his fish sticks in a sea of ketchup, either.

"Favorite color?"

"Green."

She watched as Josh scribbled the answers on one of his cards.

"Sport?"

This was a tough one. Josh was a gifted athlete, having played lots of sports in school, and he was a fierce competitor. "Jonah doesn't really do sports." She watched Josh's face fall a bit—had he already jumped to visions of a father-son game of catch? "He likes his Legos and puzzle trucks best. But he also likes to fish."

"Fish." There was an unmistakable undertone of disappointment in Josh's voice.

It shouldn't be so hard to do, but Jean felt resistance stiffen her spine even as she said, "As a matter of fact, we're going fishing this afternoon. You can come with us, if you like."

"Fishing." The single word was nearly a gulp.

Jean tried not to smile. "There's not a steep learning curve here. Even you could do it. In fact, I expect

Jonah could teach you. I'm sure we could rustle you up a pole."

Josh pursed his lips and scratched his chin. "Fishing sounds…fun. Sure, I'll come." He did not look like he considered fishing anywhere near fun, but his befuddled agreement was enjoyable to watch, indeed. He pulled another card from the holder. "What else do I need?"

Jean had no doubt that if she produced a twelve-item list, Josh would walk across the street to Bill Williams' Catch Your Match Outfitters and clean out the store's inventory. "Do you have a pair of shoes you're willing to get muddy?"

She watched him narrow one eye in contemplation of whatever footwear he'd brought. "Maybe."

"Then you're set. We've got flies, and I'll just add one more to the picnic lunch we ordered from Wanda."

He jumped on that. "Let me tackle lunch. Tackle. Lunch. Look at me. I've mastered fishing humor already."

"Okay." Jean laughed, picturing Josh negotiating picnic fare with Wanda. "Wanda has the order. Take it from there."

He pocketed the cards and rubbed his hands together, looking less like the tech magnate than she'd seen since his arrival. "Fishing. Going fishing with my son. Easy enough. I've done marketing. I know the basics of how to reel in a customer. I can do this."

Jean realized, with an amused warmth, that he was convincing himself. From behind all the doubt and anxiety, a tiny chance that they might actually work this out could be felt.

Tiny, but insistent.

Chapter Seven

Oh, dear, Jean thought to herself that afternoon as Josh walked up the street in full fisherman's regalia. *I'm going to have to have a talk with Bill Williams about ethical salesmanship.*

She'd told Josh not to buy anything. She'd told him they would find things for him to borrow. But one look at Josh told her he'd cleaned out Bill's inventory as she'd suspected he would. Right down to the top-of-the-line hip waders and what looked like the most expensive rod and reel Bill carried.

Josh tipped his "Fish Matrimony Valley" bucket cap in a comical salute. "What do you think?"

Jean swallowed a laugh and shook her head. "I think some parts of you haven't changed." If Bill thought he'd pulled one over on a city slicker, he was wrong. Sure, Josh had always been known to insist on the best equipment no matter what he did, but one look at Josh's eyes told her he knew exactly what he was doing in going overboard. This spending spree was for Jonah's—and probably Bill's—benefit, and a disobedient corner of her heart warmed at the gesture.

"I haven't had that much fun emptying my wallet in ages. Bill's a riot." Jean could just imagine Bill's smile widening with every upscale gadget Josh added to the classic multipocketed fishing vest he now wore. "We came up with two T-shirts to add to his groomsman package. What do you think of 'She'll never be the one that got away'?"

For a split second, the poignancy of that statement squeezed her heart. Did he ever think of her that way? She hadn't had time or energy to even think about dating since her return to her valley, but Josh must surely be considered at catch in his. Had there been women in his life since she left? Serious relationships? Jonah's tug at her arm, accompanied by a less-than-tactful point and giggle, left no time to ponder the thought.

She gave Jonah's hand a sharp squeeze, forcing a reprimanding look and a "Hush" finger to her lips. Impolite as it was, she couldn't really blame Jonah— Josh did look like a cartoon sales catalog version of a fly fisherman.

Instead of being insulted, it merely sent Josh into a good-natured shrug. "Too much? I was going for impressive."

She allowed herself a laugh. "I think you might have detoured to 'expensive' along the way." She caught Jonah's eye and signed, "Are you impressed?"

Rather than sign his answer, Jonah simply shook his head in a vigorous way that required no translation. He signed "silly" and "funny" with a goofy smile that let her know Jonah found these to be highly positive attributes in their new fishing companion.

"What'd he say?" The slight tone of anxious doubt in Josh's voice slid under Jean's resistance.

"He said you're silly and funny. Compliments, coming from Jonah."

Josh leaned down to Jonah's level and, to her surprise, made the sign for "Thank you."

Someone had been studying. For all the years she'd resented Josh ignoring her, she didn't know how to take his efforts at attention now. It was still classic overcompensating Josh—still the genius doing everything 150 percent and then some—but it reminded her of what it was like to have that laser-beam focus trained in her direction. When Josh Tyler paid attention to you, it was like a brilliant beam of wonder. And that beam was always enthralling—until the next thing dragged his attention elsewhere.

"Shall we head to the creek?" she said and signed at the same time.

Jonah's nod sent them on their way, Josh's squeaky new gear making a whole chorus of noises as he fell in step beside her.

She couldn't resist. "We won't really need waders where we're going, you know."

"Bill said so. But how many times does a man get to buy rubber overalls? Besides, my COO, Matt, always says when we're in deep trouble that it's 'time to get out the hip waders.' I can't wait to pull these out of my office closet next time he makes that crack."

Jean peered at the label on the waders, recognizing

the expensive brand. "Rather a high price for a joke, don't you think?"

"Some of the local businesses don't seem to be quite convinced that wedding guests will spend money here on things that aren't cakes and dresses and flowers."

It didn't take a detective to know who had groused. "Wanda gave you her standard speech?"

"Maybe. I just figured I was in a perfect position to pile a little evidence onto your campaign. Sometimes a dose of hard cash makes the point all the words in the world can't." When she looked at him, a bit stunned at his unexpected words, he gave a dismissive smile. "Win-win."

Another invasion of memory. "Win-win" was a phrase Josh used all the time. It had made their splitting up—which was a hefty dose of win-lose or even lose-lose—that much harder to accept. When she'd come home to the valley, it seemed as though everyone except Josh had lost. Her, the baby the growing inside her and then Dad.

Jonah tugged her hand, signing "know how fish?" and pointing to Josh.

"Jonah is asking if you know how to fish," she relayed.

Josh made a grave face and pinched his fingers together in the sign for "no" while shaking his head as vigorously as Jonah had earlier. "No." He looked at Jean. "Not even a little."

It pleased her that she didn't need to relay Josh's response. It pleased her even more when Jonah's chest puffed up and he signed, "I show you."

"I'll show you," she voiced Jonah's reply, a glow at her son's gentle, open spirit surging up as it always did.

Josh smiled and nodded at Jonah, then caught Jean's eyes as they continued walking. "I was hoping he'd say that."

"I never doubted it. For all the barriers he faces, Jonah doesn't see the world as full of strangers. Life here in the valley gave that to him. It's one of the reasons I'm fighting for our future."

They'd walked for a moment or two before Josh said, "San Jose is filled with strangers. Half the people I know are strangers, if that makes any sense."

It was the first admission he'd made that his California life wasn't everything they'd dreamed. She'd seen his weariness. It drew down the edges of his eyes, slumped his shoulders just a bit when he answered his continually buzzing cell phone. She was curious to see if he'd actually admit to it, if he'd trust her enough to peel back the gleam of his exceptional career.

"Are you happy?" Dad used to ask her that all the time, saying it was one of the simplest and yet most complex questions there were.

Josh looked at her, his startled expression giving way to an air of nostalgia. "You always asked questions like that."

"Nobody asks questions like that in California?"

"We're in one of the most beautiful parts of the country. We're all supposed to be happy. Or in therapy. Doesn't seem to be much room for anything in between out there." It wasn't a boast; Josh's words had a wistful quality she wouldn't have attributed to a man of his success.

"Well, as mayor of Matrimony Valley, I'll argue that I live in one of the most beautiful parts of the country."

"And are you happy?" He turned her words back on her—he was always very good at doing that.

Was she? Since Dad's death, no one else had ever asked. She considered evading the question as Josh had deftly done, but opted for honesty. "I'm content."

He exhaled. "Not always the same thing, is it?"

"A lot of people are struggling here. People who always thought the mill would be their job, that hard work would pay off and their children would have a bright future. Somehow that deal has been broken, and they're bitter. Change is hard for them."

"I didn't ask about the valley, I asked about you. Are you happy?"

"You mean do I ever regret the choice I made to stay here?"

"Well—" he shifted the fishing hat so that it hid less of his eyes "—it's all wrapped up together, isn't it?" He seemed more of a man wearing a fisherman costume than an ordinary novice fisherman—something Jonah seemed to find amusing. Every few steps Jonah would look up at his new fishing buddy and just laugh.

"True," she conceded.

"True's not an answer."

She gave him a look. "Neither is 'everyone's supposed to be happy.'"

Now it was Josh who laughed. "I never could get away with anything with you."

They'd reached her and Jonah's favorite fishing spot, and Jonah rushed forward to plunk his tiny tackle box down on the stump he always claimed as "his." Aware they had reached their destination, Josh took a moment to look around him. He gave the awed exhale she always heard from first-time visitors to spots like this—the valley could take a soul's breath away on a clear spring day. Dad, and even Grandpa, had said spots like this restored him when the strain of work and worry grew too great. "Beautiful, isn't it?"

Josh whistled. "Sure is. The California coast feels like nature showing off, you know? Dramatic vistas, crashing waves, all that. This is…"

"God telling you He's got it all covered," Jean finished for him. "Peace like a river and all that. Now you see why this has been a favorite spot of Matrims for generations."

"Matrims for generations," Josh repeated. "When my father said phrases like that, it was usually wrapped in some expectation I hadn't met. Sounds like a reassurance when you say it."

She set down the picnic basket Josh had brought over from Watson's Diner. "It is. I feel Daddy in lots of places in the valley, but here most of all. To everyone else this is Jasper Creek, but to Jonah and I this is 'Grandpa's River.'" She signed the words for "Grandpa" and "river," enjoying the smile it brought to Jonah's face.

She watched as Josh carefully imitated the signs, saying "Grandpa's river, huh?"

Jonah enthusiastically pointed his two index fingers, bumping his small fists one on top of the other as he made the sign for "Right!"

"Ha!" Josh said, giving a triumphant grin of his

own. "No translation needed there. Maybe this won't be so hard."

"Hang on there, Gizmo Guy," Jean said, amazed how easily her old nickname for Josh slipped out. "You haven't put a line in the water yet."

Gizmo Guy.

It felt like he'd been Gizmo Guy a lifetime ago. If you would have told Gizmo Guy he'd be trotting toward a mountain creek in this getup while scrambling to make conversation with his son—his *son*...the concept still shocked him to the bones—he'd never have believed it. For a man who was living out the dream he'd had since freshman year of college, some parts of life looked nothing like what he had in mind.

And Jean—she was so different from the Jean who he thought would be beside him in California, and yet she was still Jean. The soft sweetness that drew him to her back in school, that grounded him in the crazy early days of SymphoCync, was still there. She'd been crazy and adventurous back then, but there had always been a lightness and airiness to her that felt like the necessary counterbalance to the loud whiz-bang of his own personality. It struck him, as he watched her get Jonah settled with a mother's careful attention, that he'd measured every woman since against her.

And found them lacking. The few women he'd made time for—if you could call his paltry dating career that—had struck him as needy and bossy. Relationships always seemed to take more energy than they gave. Too busy to be lonely, he simply stopped trying. Not that his career didn't attract would-be girlfriends—

he could have company anytime he wanted it—it just never seemed to be worth the effort when they didn't ground him the way Jean always had.

It wasn't that he was a confirmed bachelor, it was that he was a perfectionist. Jean had felt perfect, then she was gone. Should he have gone after her? Maybe. But the fact that he hadn't just proved her point, didn't it? Still, no woman in his life had ever come as close to perfect as Jean.

Which was ironic, because now they were tethered to each other in as faulty a situation as he could imagine. Every step forward felt like choosing between less-than-perfect solutions—each option held as many marks in the "con" column as in the "pro." That was, if you could boil a child's life down into pros and cons, which he was pretty sure Jean would never condone.

He stared at the pile of gear Bill Williams had sold him, only vaguely remembering some of the how-tos Bill had provided. "So, you know how all this stuff works?" he asked Jean. She looked so at home, whereas he felt, well, like a fish out of water.

She gave his new gear a dubious look. "I know the basics. Bill would say the art of fly-fishing takes a lifetime to master."

"And yet a five-year-old can do it, so it should be within the grasp of your standard Gizmo Guy, right?" He opened the "starter kit" of twelve flies, stumped as to which one he ought to put on his line. "Which one, Jonah?"

Jean alternated loose fists up and down—the sign for "which," he guessed, and he imitated her, then held out the assortment.

With all the solemnity a five-year-old can muster, Jonah considered, then pointed to one.

"Best for whatever fish we're catching?" he asked Jean.

She laughed. "No, he just likes green."

It seemed as good a strategy as any. He smiled as he plucked the small hook with its artful display of tiny feathers and held it up. "Green it is."

The next hour was like something out of a nature documentary. The clear sky sparkled sun across the water flowing around him. His gangling, awkward attempts at casting slowly became an easier, more graceful rhythm. The slowness of it, the unhurried presentness of it, surprised him. He thought he'd be enduring an afternoon of boring fishing for the sake of spending time with his son. Instead, he found himself reveling in little details like how Jonah laughed, how the boy dangled his fingers in the water, touching the bubbling he could not hear. How deliberately he assembled his gear, even at his young age.

"You used to say you could watch me think," he ventured, unsure if it was safe to share memories of their past. "I never got it. But you can just see him think, can't you?"

Jean stared at Jonah for a long moment before answering. "Some days I can't get over how much he is like you." The softness in her voice caught him up short before she added, "Or how you were."

He didn't know how to reply to that except to say, "I'm not who I was back then. I mean I am, in some ways, but I'm different in others." He dared a look at her, squinting in the sunlight, her hair blown every which way by the breeze. "So are you."

She shrugged. "Life goes on, I suppose. I mean, look at you now." Her tone lacked the admiration people usually displayed when they said those kinds of things to him. She wasn't impressed by his success. If she felt that success had pushed her from his life, could he really blame her?

"Success is fun," he admitted. "I can buy myself anything I want."

She looked him up and down. "Clearly."

"Okay, so at times I can clean a guy's inventory out just for the fun of it. But it's a different kind of fun with Violet. I'm having a good time giving her the wedding of her dreams with all the bells and whistles, you know? Indulging her." He drew back the line and cast it again. "She doesn't know I booked one of her favorite country music artists to play the wedding reception. What's the point of owning the industry's favorite music app if you can't pull a stunt like that for your sister?"

"You always did love to show off." She nodded toward Josh's box of flies, where he'd lost two of the lures already without landing a fish. "You've got a ways to go in the fishing department, though."

Jonah, on the other hand, had landed two, but informed Josh with great seriousness that fly fishermen didn't keep their catch. Fly fishing was a catch-and-release sport—something Josh still couldn't quite get his mind around. How does a fisherman not end a fishing day with fish?

"Hey," Josh replied. "I'm just letting the little guy win."

She arched an eyebrow. "Even you can't manipulate a fish catch."

"I know," he said. "I think that's why I like it. You can't optimize it if no one's keeping score."

"Bill might argue with you there. He's always saying better equipment makes a better fisherman."

"Me and my three-hundred-dollar waders were bested by a five-year-old in green rain boots. I'm not buying it." When he realized the inadvertent pun, he laughed. "Well, actually I did buy it—all of it—didn't I?"

When their laughter settled, she turned to him. "I want to ask a favor of you."

"Anything." The ease with which he said that surprised him. In truth, he couldn't think of a single request he'd deny her at the moment.

"I'd like you to let Jonah pick a name sign for you."

"What do you mean?"

"Well, you can spell out your name—" her fingers flew through the set of gestures he'd seen her use when she first introduced him to Jonah as Mr. Josh "—but eventually most people develop a single sign that means their name. Usually, it's something about them, or something that sounds like their name, that sort of thing."

This was her way of saying Jonah would not be calling him "Dad" any time soon. She'd told him that, and he'd agreed, but the creation of a name sign seemed to underscore the point in a way that stung more than he expected.

"Sure," he agreed, less casually than he would have liked.

"I don't know what he'll come up with," she warned.

It made Josh wonder if this was some kind of test. "I'm good with whatever he chooses."

"Okay. Thanks."

The moment hung awkward between them until Jonah yelped and jumped, his fishing rod bending under what looked like a sizable catch.

"What's the sign for whopper?" Josh asked.

Her reply was almost too obvious. She spread her hands wide, then made a swimming motion with one of them. "I'd go with 'big fish.'"

Josh waded over to Jonah, making the signs followed by a comically huge "thumbs-up." He wasn't surprised when he felt his own heart expand with the size of Jonah's grin.

Chapter Eight

The afternoon seemed to wear Jonah out, so Jean and Josh shared a postfishing lemonade on her back deck as the boy napped upstairs. Bolstered by how Josh had just shared the news of Violet embracing Jonah's identity, Jean had risked moving things further by suggesting Josh join them at a church function.

It might have been going too far, for he stared at her as if she'd suggested visiting Mars. "A church potluck? Those still happen?"

"Second Sunday of every month." Given his reaction, Jean felt herself hesitate a fraction of a second before adding, "Right after the worship service." Wanting Josh to attend was a long shot of a wish—one she was almost afraid to admit—but the fishing afternoon had gone so very well and he seemed so pleased at Violet's acceptance. "It's fun," she added. "Well, maybe not the kind of fun you're used to, but you'd be surprised."

"I'm just developing a taste for fly-fishing. Surprises aren't surprising me so much anymore." Josh stuffed his hands into his pockets. "Only, I don't cook. Aren't I supposed to bring something to a potluck?"

She'd already thought of a way around that and nodded toward the pitcher on the table between them. "But you can mix lemonade."

Jean was pleased to see him grin. "Yeah, but…" His face grew a bit more serious. "Church service?"

She'd wondered if he'd accept that part of the invitation. "They set up the tables on the church lawn right after. You don't have to go if you don't…feel comfortable. You can meet me and Jonah outside afterward."

Jean watched him ponder the possibility. "I haven't been inside a church since Dad's funeral."

She offered him the only persuasion she had. "It's nice. Peaceful. I don't think I could make it through the week without the grounding I get there." The unmoored look hadn't ever really left his eyes while he'd been here, and the vision of her standing in a church pew with Jonah on one side and Josh on the other called to her with a power she wasn't ready to admit. "You might find you like it." She wished she hadn't said that. It felt silly and pushy. She turned and fiddled with a plant from one of the deck containers rather than let Josh see whatever pleading might be in her eyes.

"What time?"

She looked up. "Ten thirty. Lunch starts just before noon."

"And you're sure stirring lemonade is enough to get me in without being a potluck moocher?"

She'd have to pass that phrase on to the chair of the church social committee. "There are no moochers, just guests. There's always enough food to feed twice whoever's there anyways. You'll just be helping to even out the ratio."

"Well." He laughed. "When you put it that way, I don't see how I can refuse." He looked around the backyard. "You've got a nice thing here, Jean. A good place for a boy like Jonah to grow up."

His praise warmed her heart more than a hundred perfect wedding reviews. She needed him to understand what she was doing here, why it was so essential that the valley keep being the home it was. For her and for Jonah. That—not some need to launch a bridal empire—is what drove her to shed the family name off the valley and the falls. Could a man so steeped in enterprise and so bereft of family ties see that? Was he capable of appreciating such goals?

"I need the valley to go on," she said. "I need to know it will be here for Jonah. I suppose it's how I hold up my piece of Dad and Grandpa's legacy."

"Even without the Matrim name?"

"It was never about that. I suppose that's hard for you to understand."

"No," he said, his expression warming. "I get it. I feel the same way about SymphoCync, actually, I love the product, and success is nice, but it's the people inside the big shiny building that keep me up nights. I like what I've built, but I really like who I've built it with—if that makes any sense."

That surprised her. "Really?"

He gave her a look. "Is that so hard to believe?"

"Yes, actually." She'd seen him make fast, efficient phone calls, verbal checklists devoid of the small talk and personal inquiries that made doing business in the valley such a pleasure. She remembered how achievements topped his to-do list far more often than relationships did. He had always lived at too fast a speed to foster any real connections. "I don't see how you can do business at the speed of light like you do and pay any attention to people and their lives."

He flinched, with a dramatic hand to his chest. "Ouch. Stop holding back and tell me how you really feel, Your Honor."

She crossed her arms. If she'd stepped out onto this thin ice, she was going to walk on it until it cracked. "How many people work at SymphoCync?"

"Eighty-two. We still classify as a start-up."

It would take more people than that to pull off each wedding in the valley. Which was ironic, when Jean figured how much he likely earned compared with how small Matrimony Valley was, incomewise. Dad's old comment about God's economy turning the world's economy upside down rang in her head. It was time to see if he really had changed. "Okay, then, name five of your employees' children."

"Pete in accounting has two girls...one starts with an N... Hal's wife had twins last summer—I remember we lost him right before a launch when he rushed out of the office in a state of panic when she texted she was in labor. And... Roger has two kids, maybe three. One of them is Roger Junior, I know that."

She could name every child in the valley, as could most of the residents. To her, that was the best part of the community—everyone knew everyone else. "I rest my case." She tried not to let her voice show her disappointment.

"Hey, just because I don't hoard details doesn't mean I don't care."

"You may care, Josh, but details like that are the way you *show* it. It takes time and attention to care about people. People are complicated and inefficient. They mess with your timetables and—" she looked straight at him "—they show up out of the blue after years."

Josh huffed and scratched his chin. "I still can't get over this. I mean, what are the odds?"

She sighed. "I don't know why God chose now to bring you back to the valley. I sure wouldn't have picked this timing."

"Come on, we both know it was Violet who brought me to the valley. I'm not ready to sign on to the concept that I'm here by divine intervention. I mean, I'll come to service because you asked and all, but..."

"But what? Your stunning scientific brain can't accept the idea of God moving in the world, of God bringing Jonah's father into his life?" If the crazy set of circumstances that brought Josh into the valley didn't show God's hand to this man, what on earth could ever convince him? How could someone so brilliant deny something so clear?

"You mean the idea of God doing what Jonah's mother wouldn't?" Josh's words were cut with the sharp edges of that first day. The fact that he'd said "Jonah's mother" instead of just saying "you" cut twice as deep.

The idea that Josh's arrival was indeed a conviction of that mistake had kept her up more than one night. Was God doing what she wouldn't? The fine line between providence and punishment felt sharp enough to slice her heart in two. She had no right to pass judgment on who Josh was now, but he had every right to hold her silence against her. Could they ever get past all the hurt in their history to give Jonah two real parents? What were "real parents" anyway? Given the present circumstances, could she and Josh even come close?

Maybe step one was to own up and apologize. Jean took a deep breath. "Keeping Jonah from you was wrong. I know that, now. Maybe someday you can forgive me for what I thought was a good decision at the time. For Jonah's sake, if not for mine."

Josh got up and walked to the edge of the deck. "I don't want to fight, Jean. This is hard enough without you and me going at each other."

That's why I need to go to church, she wanted to say, but stayed silent. This situation was so wrought with the need for grace and mercy, she couldn't imagine wading through it without the faith that God knew the outcome.

"Please come," she said quietly. "It will mean so much to Jonah. He's chosen a name sign for you, and he wants to use it to introduce you around at the potluck."

The news had the effect she'd hoped; Josh's face softened. "What is it?"

"That's not for me to say." She ventured a small smile. "But I think you'll like it."

He held her eyes for a moment, and the connection renewed her spark of hope that this could all work out. Maybe they could get to the place where they could forgive one other for the hurts they'd each inflicted. Maybe she could trust that God knew just what Jonah needed even better than she did.

"Then I've got to come," he replied.

* * *

A clanging tone startled Josh awake that night. The room was dark and unfamiliar, lit only by the screen of the laptop open on the bed beside him. He blinked at the cheerful man in the video sign language course on the screen, his half-awake brain straining to remember his surroundings. The phone clanged again, and the irritating collection of electronic tones sent Josh scrambling through the linens until he found his phone where it had fallen on the floor.

"Tyler here," he groaned into the phone as he righted himself from the contortions needed to reach down from the high antique bed.

"What is going on out there?" Matt's voice held a touch of alarm. "You send me an email saying you're staying out there and don't call?"

"Hey, Matt." Josh sat up, squinting his eyes to see the 2:00 a.m. eastern time signature on his computer screen. He'd expected this call much earlier after the message he'd sent, now regretting the slightly cowardly tactic of opting for email instead of a phone call or text. "It's the middle of the night here, you know."

"It's only eleven here, and you get no points for consideration at the moment. I was starting to think my airlift joke from the other day wasn't so funny. What's going on? Taking the weekend? You don't take weekends. We're two weeks into a launch, you have that big speech on Tuesday—the next ten days are huge for us. What's with the sudden need for R & R?"

Josh snapped on the light and reached for the half-empty glass of soda on the nightstand. "Everything going okay?"

"The launch is going fine, actually, but that's not an excuse to disappear on me." Matt had every right to be annoyed, but his words also held an air of concern. "Don't pull a stunt like this. What's going on? What's with a three-sentence email saying you're staying the weekend instead of coming home?"

Letting his head fall back against the high carved headboard, Josh replied, "Well, how much time you got? This has about a three-hour explanation." The familiar creak Josh heard told him Matt was settling back in his desk chair. "You're still at the office."

"We're in launch mode. I'm spending my Saturday night sleeping at the office because the other member of upper management seems to have gone fishing."

If only Matt knew how spot-on he was. "I'm sorry to leave you hanging. This is all just a bit…weird… right now."

"Weird? You mean with Mayor Jean?"

The issue of Mayor Jean seemed almost simple compared with the whole, newly complicated, picture. "That's part of it."

"And what's the other part?"

"The boy. The one on the website." Josh swallowed. "He's my son." The three words still felt like they were made of concrete every time he forced them out.

There was a stunned silence on the other end of the line, followed by keys tapping, then a low whistle. "The kid…is yours? Oh, man, I can see it now. He does look like you. But that doesn't mean for sure. There are tests for that sort of thing, Josh."

"Jean isn't lying to me, Matt. Jonah is my son."

"You never knew? Really? Why on earth wouldn't she tell you?"

He thought about what she'd said earlier this evening. Yes, he disagreed with her choice, but he also knew he'd given her plenty of reasons to doubt him. After all, she'd come back here even before she knew she was carrying his child. Besides, did it really make sense now to try to place blame? "There's a lot to it. There are complicated reasons."

"What do you mean?"

Josh recalled the mother-bear fierceness in Jean's eyes. *He's not broken, Josh. He's perfect the way he is, just different.* "Jonah is deaf." He felt compelled to add, "He's not defective. He's amazing."

"So you've met?"

"Not as his dad. Jean isn't sure he's ready for that quite yet. But I spent some time with him Friday, and I went fishing with him today..." He yawned with another glance at the clock. "...well, yesterday."

"You're kidding. So the fishing crack—who knew? But, um, do you know how to fish?"

Josh managed a weary laugh. "I do now. I also know how to say fourteen different things in sign language I didn't know yesterday."

"You should have told me. I should have known this was happening."

It had been a foolish move not to call Matt and talk it out. This whole business had messed with his head. "I'm sorry. And believe me, I'd be no good to you right now. My brain is in knots. I'll get on a flight tonight." The words tasted sour in his mouth. His reluctance to get on that plane stunned and worried him. "I just... I needed another day or two to figure this out, you know?"

"You're a dad. I'm sitting here, staring at the photo, and I still can't get my head around it."

"Try it from my end. I don't know what to do here, Matt. I don't know how I'm supposed to act or what I'm supposed to say or how I tell him who I am. But I want him to hear it from me. Well, from Jean and me I suppose, but I want to say the words to him. Or sign the words, or however you do this…" The whole situation seemed to swallow him like the utter black quiet of the night out here.

"Hey" came Matt's voice. "I know it's big, but I'm sure you can handle this."

Josh let his head fall back against the bed. "I'm not."

"Well, yeah, you just left your second-in-command hanging without an explanation. So maybe you don't have it figured out quite yet. But you will."

"I hope you're right."

"Look, I get that you're a bit thrown by this, but you know what's at stake out here. Tuesday's presentation is going to set our whole next year. This is launch, Josh—crunch time for you to be out there selling SymphoCync. You can't do that from some tiny mountain town, you've got to be here."

"I know." Hearing his own weak tone, he repeated, "I know," more forcefully, even though he didn't feel it.

"Okay, then. Text me your flight time and I'll pick you up from the airport myself."

Josh couldn't be sure if the offer was made out of friendship or enforcement. SymphoCync needed him. He owed his loyalty to the company he'd built.

Only now, another loyalty divided him. More sharply than he'd ever expected.

Chapter Nine

Jean recounted the whole comical scene of Jonah's "big fish" with Josh as she sat on Kelly's back steps Sunday morning before church. As single mothers, Jean and Kelly alternated bringing each other coffee and goodies before Sunday service in an unofficial support group. "Mom's Night Out" wasn't a luxury either of them could afford very often, so "Mom's Sunday Coffee" served as a creative stand-in.

"It was quite a scene. I think Josh was wearing every piece of fishing gear Bill stocked. I know he did it to impress Jonah, and that's sweet, but he looked ridiculous."

Kelly smiled and waved at her daughter, Lulu, who was pushing Jonah on a swing. "It is sweet. And not cheap." She lowered her voice, even though the children were several yards away. "Did you know Jonah's father was so successful?"

Jean picked up a leaf off the steps, turning it to catch the morning sunshine. "Sort of. I mean, it was clear while we were out there that Josh would do big things, and I followed his career for a while until it didn't make sense to keep pricking myself on that thorn. The life Josh lives consumed him. I felt like it made me invisible. So I decided I'd rather have none of his attention than have to beg for whatever was left over from SymphoCync. It seemed the right choice then. Now, I'm coming to see how much that choice hurt him. Hurt all of us, really."

"And then he shows up on your doorstep." Kelly leaned back, propping her elbows on the step above. "Seriously, Jean, you have to believe God's up to something. Even if I believed in coincidences—which I don't—this one's too much of a reach to be anything but God."

Jean had come to the same unsettling conclusion. "I know Josh is Jonah's father. And I know it might not have been a perfect choice to keep that from him. I've made a bunch of imperfect choices in my life. But that's exactly why I don't want to make a bad one now. I don't know what kind of father Josh will be to Jonah. I don't think even Josh knows what kind of father he wants to be. It could all go so horribly wrong."

Kelly gave Jean a look. "Or it could all go so wonderfully right. I mean, the guy's going out on a limb— or is it out into the creek, in this case? He's letting you call the shots, letting you set the pace for how and what Jonah knows, right?"

"Not entirely. He wants Jonah to know who he is. Right now. But I'm just not ready. If Jonah sees Josh as his father, and then Josh leaves..."

"Hey, I'm on your side here. You're protecting your son, and that's a good thing. But this isn't a new relationship—Josh is already Jonah's father. You've just got to figure out how to factor that into Jonah's life in the best way possible."

Jean rested her head on her hand. "And what way is that?"

"I'm not the answer lady. I'm just the flower lady. But I do know that if some handsome West Coast tech exec turned his schedule upside down to stay a couple of extra days to get to know the son he never knew he had, I'd pay attention. I'd be shooting for cautiously optimistic."

"At the moment, I'm settling for thoroughly confused."

"Well, there's that, too." Kelly wrapped a comforting arm around Jean as Lulu giggled at a face Jonah made. "How do you feel about the whole thing? About him?"

"I'm still in shock, I think. And I feel guilty for keeping such a secret, I suppose. I could have told Josh. I could have stood up to his father. I could have believed he would stand up to his father."

Kelly chose a doughnut from the bag she had brought. "Done all that *and* raised a special needs son?" She broke off a piece. "*And* dealt with your father's health? *And* fought for Josh's attention and defense while he was out playing tech tycoon? Don't be so hard on yourself. You chose your battles while you were outnumbered. Jonah's had a happy, loving life because of it. That life is just going to get a bit more complicated now."

Jean gave a resigned laugh as she chose her own doughnut. "A bit?"

"Okay, maybe a lot. I'm just saying there could be

some good coming with all that complication." Kelly ate the piece of doughnut before continuing. "You still haven't answered my question."

"I told you. I feel guilty. Scared. Worried."

"I meant the part about him. You and Josh have some serious history together. He's the father of your child. You were in love with him, were willing to marry him. What are you feeling now?"

Jean hid in her coffee cup, taking a long swallow while she figured out how on earth to answer the question. "I'm feeling a million different things. He's the same Josh I knew—brilliant, mesmerizing, dashing— but different. In some ways he's still laser focused, and then in other ways he seems… I don't know…drifting. Unsettled. Like the foundation is coming out from underneath him—which is a perfectly human reaction for a man who's just discovered he's a father, I suppose." She dunked her doughnut in her coffee. "I threw him a monster of a curve, I know that."

"And he could have balked. He could have done a lot of things other than try to make a connection with Jonah the way he has." She sighed. "This parenting stuff is hard alone. You know that. Even having him as just a bit of a partner is going to help, don't you think?"

Jean set down the coffee. "That's just it, I'm not so sure. I want Jonah to have a real daddy in his life. The kind that will show up at baseball games and help with homework and *be there*. How can Josh ever be that? Jonah's idea of 'father' will always be fractured now. That makes me sad."

Kelly swallowed. "Maybe fractured beats none at all."

Jean wanted to bite her thoughtless tongue. Kelly had lost her husband in an aviation accident two years ago when Lulu was six. Kelly fought every day to keep Lulu's memories of her father alive. "I'm sorry, Kelly. That was a lousy thing for me to say. How can I sit here and gripe about Josh coming back like this? Mark can never come back for you or for Lulu."

Kelly blinked hard, her voice thick with emotion. "Well, this side of Heaven at least." She ran a finger down a section of deck railing. "You've got a chance here. Maybe only for Jonah, but maybe for you, too. Take it from a girl who's lost her chances. This one might be worth taking."

"You mean me? With Josh?"

Kelly pointed at Jean. "Don't tell me you haven't thought about it. Come on. Money, looks, over-the-top daddy antics? I know I'd be thinking about it."

"He's got no faith, Kelly. That man's spiritual side lives inside a computer case. Or his checkbook. Or nowhere. No thanks, I'm not in the market for that."

"But you just said he seemed unsettled to you. Maybe God's shaking up more than Jonah's parentage. It's good marketing, when you think about it."

Jean balked. "What on earth do you mean?"

"What does it say about a town called Matrimony Valley if we can't pair off our own mayor?" Kelly stood up and called to the children. "Lulu, bring Jonah in to wash up. Church starts in thirty minutes." She winked at Jean. "And we can't be late this morning, can we?"

They were all staring at him, right? The pretender from California infiltrating the sanctity of a humble mountain congregation. The guy who wasn't even sure God was out there sitting among all these people who seemed to think God was close. Friendly. Comfortable, even.

The church was impressive in its unimpressiveness—if that made any sense. It had pretty stained windows and arches that graced the ceiling as rows of pews filled the floor. It was pleasant enough to look at, but that wasn't at all what made the place so memorable. The warmth of the space—a warmth that had nothing to do with the May morning—wouldn't let him leave despite the imposter impulse that kept him glancing back at the door.

Still, when he looked around, no one did anything but smile at him. And then there was the singing. The hymns that had been sung at Dad's funeral were mostly done by impressive soloists with a thin smattering of voices joining in from the congregation. In this church, everyone sang, and sang loud—even the guy behind him who had less of a sense of pitch than Josh had. By the end of the second hymn, Josh ventured a quiet bar or two and didn't feel embarrassed at all by his lack of talent. As a matter of fact, Jean smiled and sang with a little more enthusiasm herself. And Jonah? He "sang" in his own way, zealously waving hands as if conducting some imaginary orchestra. The whole thing captured him.

But how? He was in church. In Jean Matrim's church. And it didn't feel weird. New, maybe. Startling for sure, but not weird in a "you don't belong" sense. In fact, Josh had the inexplicable sense that he *could* belong here. That the people around him would let him belong—*welcome* him, even—if he so chose. As if all the missteps of his past and all his shortcomings wouldn't bar him from entry, but just make him like everybody else who sought comfort and solace from this place.

He tried to follow along with the service, but mostly struggled to keep his focus despite the rush of awareness that seemed to come at him from all sides. He kept waiting for the bubble to pop, for the impossible warmth and welcome to evaporate, but it never did.

Sincere. That was the improbable word that kept thumping in his brain. The faith here, in this place and in this town, was sincere. Real. He knew lots of people who claimed to have the wondrous sort of grounded peace he felt here, but this was the first place he actually thought it might exist. And even though he wasn't at all sure he had a shot at having such a faith, it sure was nice to just sit here and bask in it for an hour.

An hour that seemed to be up as fast as it began, and Josh wanted to blink and shake his head to clear it as he filed out of the church with Jean and Jonah and the other congregants. Several of them he had met during his short time here. There were older ladies in hats Violet would classify as "vintage." There were older men in starched clean shirts and suspenders. In fact, there were people of every age: some in their late twenties like himself, some older, gawky teenagers, fidgeting kids and cooing babies. It was like a slice of the whole country boiled down into one little pot where everyone called everyone else by name.

The whole experience was so far from the coffee-bar-power-brunch kind of Sunday morning he'd known in San Jose that it wasn't hard to realize there were thousands of miles between the two.

It wasn't just the inside of the church. The whole valley was intensely green—plants and blooms seemed to erupt from every square inch, as if the town was barely holding back the mountainside from its march toward the Atlantic on the other side of the state. Droughts had reduced California's landscape into a palate of browns and tans that made him treasure the loud city colors. Now, the neon combinations felt forced next to how the colors here naturally fit together.

Surely, Jean would make some remark about the beauty of God's creation if he voiced such thoughts. In this morning's service, as the little church organ pumped out accompaniments to heartily sung hymns, Josh found he wouldn't argue.

He couldn't deny it: there really was something about the valley. He wanted to stay longer, even though he couldn't. He'd stretched his absence to the limit, and still an annoyingly large part of him would be sorry to get on that plane today. That regret was partly due to Jonah, partly due to the place itself and partly due to Jean. Actually, it felt more than partly due to Jean. All those parts were adding up to too much, and he didn't know what to do with that.

"I expect you're used to something a bit slicker than our little congregation," Pastor Ryan Mitchell said as he shook Josh's hand at the church entrance after the service.

"I'm not used to anything at all," Josh admitted, regretting the puzzled look that brought to the pastor's face. "This has its charms," he backpedaled, not wanting to admit his lack of faith. "I enjoyed it." He had—surprising as that was.

"Well, you're sure to enjoy what comes next," Mitchell said, gesturing to the spread of folding tables covered in brightly colored tablecloths. "Best meals there are, our potlucks."

"So Jean tells me."

Jonah tugged on Jean's arm, then flurried through a sequence of signs. Jean laughed and replied with the nodding fist Josh now knew meant "yes," after which Jonah took off into the crowd of children like any other young boy would do.

"He do okay this morning?" the pastor asked Jean.

"Wiggly, but that's to be expected," Jean replied.

"Jonah's teacher, Gina, spends the weekends down in Asheville with her mama, so we get an interpreter in here once a month," the pastor explained to Josh. "I wish it were more often—it ought to be more—but that's the best we can do for Jonah right now. I've learned the basics like everybody else in town, but it isn't enough."

"You do a great job. If I'd been Jonah, I'd think the whole service was just for me," Josh replied. He'd been impressed at the number of signs the pastor had worked into his service—certainly enough to convey the essentials to a young brain.

"It is just for you. It's just for each of us. I always say the air between my mouth and your ears is holy ground. What you get out of service is Spirit work, son, not cleverness on my part."

What *did* he get out of the service? He was still

working that out. He was still working out a lot of things.

"I've got to get my salad fixings out of the car," Jean interrupted. "And that lemonade duty's going to start in a minute, so you'd best get stirring."

That brought a laugh from the pastor. "Her Honor get you working already? I thought you were just a guest."

"Mayor Jean gets everybody working, doesn't she?" Josh replied. He walked off toward the table set with a dozen pitchers of water and an enormous can of lemonade mix, not liking how the words *just a guest* sat wrong in his gut.

Bill Williams came up to help just as Josh was scooping the last of the mix into the final pitcher. "How'd all your gear work? Good fishing?"

"Well, I can almost cast without endangering everyone around me," Josh said with a laugh. "But I look the part, that's for sure."

"Fake it to make it, I always say." He leaned close. "Any fisherman will tell you it's never about the catch anyway. Mostly just gives a man time to think. Life doesn't leave much time for that these days, especially out where you're from."

Jean came up from behind Bill. "You done good, Bill. I saw our friend here go a whole hour without checking his cell phone. That's not like the Josh I knew."

Her eyes widened for just a second as she realized her slip. Josh stepped in to cover. "Jean and I actually went to the same college. Small world, huh?"

"Seems so," said Bill. "And now you'll be walking Miss Violet down the aisle as our first bride." The man gave Jean the same warm smile that made Josh like him in the first place. "Fine thing Jean's done for the valley." He touched her shoulder with a fatherly air. "Your daddy'd be busting his buttons with pride if he were here, hon. I expect you know that."

Jean's eyes teared up a bit, and her cheeks pinked in a way Josh felt tingle under his skin. "I do, Bill, I do."

Without asking if Josh needed any help, Bill simply took two of the mixed pitchers and walked over to set them on the nearest tables. "He gave Jonah a toy fishing game for his second birthday," Jean said as she looked after the man. "It was Jonah's first birthday with Dad gone, and Bill just appeared on our doorstep with the whole thing, big blue bow and all, saying how birthdays were important to little boys." Jean's voice was thick with emotion.

Josh had received a dozen texts on his last birthday, a handmade card from Violet and a few offers for rounds of drinks after work that he didn't have time to accept. "Is Bill that nice to everyone?"

"Mostly," Jean said, "but I think he has a soft spot for Jonah because he and Rose lost their own son in Afghanistan three years ago. Rusty had the same birthday as Jonah." Her voice went soft and quiet. "Bill and Dad were fishing buddies. He and Rose have been great to me and Jonah, really." Jean held his eyes for a moment, loss and memory glistening there in the threat of tears. Then she straightened herself in the way he'd seen her do so often, and grabbed two pitchers herself. "Well, I don't know about you, but I'm hungry. Let's get this lemonade on the tables so we can get you fed before you hop on that plane."

Josh stopped her. "What day is Jonah's birthday?" It seemed such a sorry thing that he didn't know and hadn't yet thought to ask.

"August 10." She said the words with importance.

Josh looked at her for a long moment before he promised, "I won't forget. Ever."

He wanted her to smile and say, "I know you won't," but she simply smiled, nodded and walked toward the table with the lemonade.

Chapter Ten

Jean felt as if her insides whirled. Today was supposed to make a happy end to the surprise entrance of Josh into her life. Instead, Josh's presence in the service and beside her at a "family" event like the Sunday potluck just churned old and new feelings up together in an unsettling torrent.

Not that anyone was making assumptions—most of the valley presumed she was paying special attention to the members of the first bridal party. Yes, a few eyebrows rose in question—Josh was a very handsome single man, after all. Kelly hadn't been the first to hint that Matrimony Valley ought to be able to offer up a match for its mayor someday. It was the full history she and Josh shared, though, that gave the day such weight. Not only the history, but the uncertainty of the future. Josh belonged in Jonah's life, she could see that now. It was just how, and how much, that she couldn't predict.

Jonah ran up to her as she set down the pitcher of lemonade at the table. "Now?" he signed, pointing at

Josh, who was finishing up distributing the last of the lemonade.

Jonah was a friendly child by nature, but even that gregarious spirit didn't explain the connection her son felt with the man who was his father. It made her wonder, over the past few days, if the whole world couldn't see the relationship between them. Their near-instant connection and physical similarities shouted out to her—could everyone see it so easily?

"OK," she signed as she saved a seat on the other side of Jonah for Josh. Jonah was so eager to give Josh his name sign that it made her second-guess withholding Josh's true title from her son. It wasn't wrong to protect the boy from heartbreak until she knew Josh would stay in his life, was it? The loss of his grandfather was loss enough—she'd spare him any further hurt any way she could.

Josh laughed as Jonah tugged him enthusiastically to the place setting and tapped both small hands on the chair in an invitation to sit.

"As you can see, Jonah's very ready to present you with your name sign," Jean explained.

"I get that," Josh replied, making a big show of sitting down as instructed. "You could have let him do it earlier, you know."

"And miss my best leverage for good church behavior?" she replied with a laugh and a wink at Jonah. "A mom needs to use any advantage she's got." She caught Jonah's eye and signed, "Now you may," while voicing the same words.

"Wait—" Josh cut in, twisting to face Jonah. Slowly he said, "Jonah, what is my name?" while executing the corresponding signs with fumbling but enthusiastic fingers.

Jean's heart turned over in her chest at the effort. The moment suddenly felt hugely important for all three of them.

Jonah grinned wildly and made the combined sign he'd chosen, wiggling the fingers on both hands back and forth in a "swimming" motion as he gradually separated his palms in front of his chest.

Josh paid careful attention, his eyebrows furrowing in an effort to connect the sign he'd seen before, finally looking to Jean for an explanation. The eagerness she saw in those dark eyes turned her heart over again. "Wait, I'm…?"

"Big Fish," she said as Jonah made the sign again.

As name signs go, it was unusual. Then again, was there anything even close to ordinary in the situation? For a moment, Jean held her breath, uncertain of Josh's reaction.

Josh's eyes widened for a moment, and then he threw his head back and laughed. "Big Fish!" he repeated, imitating the sign as Jonah made it again. "I love it. Big Fish. My name is Big Fish." Without any instruction from her, he'd used the signs from his earlier question so that he could form the sentence "My name is Big Fish."

"Yes!" Jonah signed with a happy yelp that erupted into nonstop giggles.

"Big Fish." Josh repeated it like the grandest of titles, wiggling his "fishy" fingers with delight.

Bill and Rose, who had taken seats on the far side of the table and had seen the exchange, laughed. "Hello there, Big Fish," Bill said, trying the name out on his own fingers. "Nice to meet you." Bill caught Jonah's attention and signed "Well done!" as he said the same.

"Thank you," Jonah signed back.

Josh touched Jonah's shoulder, signing, "Thank you." She could hear the powerful emotion in his voice. She'd worried he would take offense at whatever name Josh chose, aware that it served as a barrier to his true identity. His delight at being named "Big Fish" was as heartwarming as it was surprising. She had no doubt that Josh would be introduced to every person on the lawn before the day was over.

Jonah waved at Kelly, who'd seated herself across the table from Jean as a sign of moral support, and signed "My friend Big Fish" to her.

Kelly's smile was filled with understanding, and she signed back, "Good choice."

"Take your seats, everyone, while I say a blessing over our meal" came Pastor Mitchell's voice.

Bill and Rose, unaware of the weight of the moment they'd just witnessed, joined hands and reached out to Kelly and Josh, as well. And there they were, joined in a circle of hands, Jonah unaware he held the hands of each of his parents in his two small fists.

She felt the moment hit her like a landslide, somehow deeply aware of how it hit Josh, as well. Pastor Mitchell's words washed over her, heard but barely understood over the roar of emotions in her chest. How could she have any hope of going back to a life that didn't include Josh now? How could she hold back the bursts of optimism that he would truly be part of their lives? Those insistent bursts waged war with the protective mama side of her that would not, *could not*, see Jonah hurt or ignored or sidelined by the man her son had proclaimed "Big Fish."

Oh, Father, she prayed silently alongside Pastor Mitchell's mealtime blessing. *Protect us. So much could go wrong here.*

Yet, for the first time since Josh Tyler had set foot in Matrimony Valley, Jean began to believe there might be a chance for so much to go right.

Bill Williams caught up with him at the dessert table. "So you'll be back for the wedding?"

"Of course," Josh replied. "And who knows? I might need more gear by then."

Bill laughed. "I expect a man like you can get a whole load of top-notch stuff on the internet."

"I could." Josh smiled in return. "But I've discovered I like the old-school approach. Go ahead and see what you can whip up for me for when I come back."

Bill scratched his chin. "Oh, I don't know that you'll have much time to fish with all that wedding stuff going on. Jean's got so much happening, I feel like she ought to post a calendar on a sign in the middle of the street."

"She's organized, I'll give her that." Josh gazed over at Jean, talking to a knot of people on the far side of the lawn.

"She's more than that. She's a lot like her daddy. I'm thinking she saved the valley. Pretty special, that one." He shot Josh a look. "I'm thinking maybe you see that, too." When Josh raised an eyebrow, he went on. "You didn't go home with your sister the other day."

"Wow, I guess what they say about small towns is true," Josh replied, feeling a flush rise up his neck. "Everybody's watching everybody."

Bill stuffed his hands in his pockets and rocked back on his heels. "We got our charms and our faults, just like the rest of the world." After a moment, he added, "You're welcome back anytime, you know. Don't have to be for the wedding stuff. You can come just 'cause you want to." He nodded toward Jean. "To fish, that is."

Jean stood before Josh in the airport terminal drive later that Sunday afternoon. She'd left Jonah with Bill and Rose, aware this farewell would be difficult and awkward. "I owe you an apology," she began.

Josh shifted his bag to his other hand. "I thought we were past that now."

She fiddled with the drawing she held. "No, I owe you an apology for something else." She felt she had to say this, had to get it out on the chance it really would be years before she'd see him again. Which was silly—he'd be returning for Violet's wedding a dozen days from now—but the irrational fear stuck in her gut anyway. "I...well, I misjudged you."

"I don't understand."

"We weren't...perfect...when we were together, but I put that all on you. In my mind, I built you into this distant, busy executive. Someone too much like your father. It was easier on me, I think, to view you that way. To make it all about how you wouldn't listen and none of it about how I wouldn't make you understand. Part of the fault for what happened between us falls to me. On my unwillingness—then—to stand up for myself. I made you the bad guy because that made it easier to stay away, to keep the silence between us."

"Well," he said, "it's not like I didn't give you reasons to think that way." He shifted his weight. "I didn't pay attention. I took you for granted. And that falls on me. I don't want to be that kind of man anymore."

She dared a long look into his eyes, pleased to see sincerity there. "For what it's worth, I do believe you aren't that man anymore."

"I'm not—well, I don't want to be." The strength of his gaze tilted her off balance, the dazzle both familiar and a bit frightening. "This isn't the last time you're going to see me." The way his voice could pull her in hadn't faded with time.

"Of course not," she countered, scrambling for the distance she was quickly losing. "The wedding's coming."

"That's not what I meant. Look, I don't know how we make this work, but I do know we *will* make this work. I won't be the 'Big Fish' that got away."

It was just like Josh to find a clever way to say the really important stuff. She admired clever, but she needed true. She knew what his powers of persuasion could do to her, knew her doubts were still warranted. After only four days, could she truly believe Josh's attentions would stick? Could she really count on it? Especially with Jonah's heart on the line?

"I'm having my office send Jonah a new electronic tablet. This one has built-in video and transcription software. When I talk, it will write the words out in captions on the screen. That way, when I goof up on the signs, you can still tell him what I mean. And I'm going to get fluent in emoji, too, so we can talk in those tiny pictures in addition to whatever words he can read at his age."

"That's really kind of you." He was trying so hard. Jean felt her heart tug madly after the fact, too desperate to believe this first burst of enthusiasm would last. It was just that all the years of "old Josh" weren't allowing her to stake so much on the "new Josh" she'd met this week.

"He's amazing, Jean. Just the way he is, just like you said. You've done an incredible job. I..." He didn't finish the thought—something that wasn't like him. Josh Tyler finished every thought, usually with a flourish.

"You have a plane to catch," she made herself say. "Don't forget your 'Big Fish' drawing."

He smiled at the paper. "I've never had a drawing to put on my fridge before. I'm not even sure I have those magnets you use to hold them there."

"You'll adapt." How had he managed to look even more attractive now than he did earlier today at the potluck? Confidence looked wonderful on this man, but the unsettled look in his eyes right now went straight to her heart in a way his trademark confidence never had.

"I'm glad, you know," he admitted with an uncharacteristic sheepishness. "I'm glad I wound up here. Violet says it's fate, but I know you have a different opinion."

Jean took a deep breath. "I'm thankful God brought you to the valley. I'm..." She was going to go ahead and say it, even though it felt like hurtling over the falls. "I'm thankful you're back in our lives." She'd said "our lives" and not just "Jonah's life." His eyes widened, and suddenly the exposure of the admission felt like too much. "I'm glad Jonah will know his father."

He paused a long moment before replying, "That, too." He took a step toward her. "You know, I never really stopped wondering how you were doing. Maybe not enough to act on it, and that's on me, but I did think of you." Josh smiled, shaking his head. "Mayor Jean Matrim. Pretty impressive."

She waved away his compliment, wishing he wouldn't stand close enough for her to smell the elegant beachy-spicy aftershave, or be pulled in by the depths of his brown eyes. "Oh, I doubt you're impressed by the likes of Matrimony Valley."

"I am. The valley, and its mayor." Before she could stop him, he leaned in and left the lightest of kisses on her cheek. "See you soon."

All those years and all this baggage didn't change how he could still blow her away with the slightest touch. She coughed, fighting to wrench her composure back by saying, "Memorial Day weekend." That was Violet's wedding weekend.

"Before that. Maybe in person, but at least online. Gotta show off my new sign skills as I learn them, right?" He duplicated the name sign he hadn't stopped repeating since the potluck. "Big Fish and all."

"Big Fish." Josh had never once mentioned what she could see in his eyes: he knew, just as she did, that Big Fish was just a placeholder until she allowed him to use Daddy.

"I'm glad you like it."

"I figured it'd just be some jazzed-up version of Josh, but this is *much* better." He grinned. "I wonder if I can make them put it as my title on my business cards. I mean, CEO is impressive, but Big Fish is so memorable."

Was he going out of his way to show her he was okay with the fact that it wasn't Dad? Did he really just genuinely get a kick out of Jonah's choice? Jean couldn't tell. She could barely think straight about anything today. A host of different emotions tossed her off balance. She couldn't ignore the warm glow of the attraction Josh could still pull from her.

But neither could she ignore the dark wall of fear and doubt over what their future held. She'd never be able to *make* him pay attention to his son or to her. If he *chose* to, it might truly work. But even if he had the best of intentions toward them, the demands of his life were loud and relentless. She'd welcome his promises, accept his declarations, but she'd never allow herself to count on them. All of this week's progress didn't change how much forgiveness they still had to work through with each other.

He put his hand to his forehead as if he knew that, as well. "I've got a million things I want to say. A million conversations I want to have. Only I can't find a way to start any of them just yet." He made a frustrated sound. "We need so much more time than we've had."

Jean made herself stare straight at him, even though her heart was turning rebellious cartwheels inside her chest. "So come back."

"I will. I really will."

Too much of her wanted to believe him. Far more than was safe just yet.

He must have seen the resistance in her eyes because he grabbed her hand. "No, I mean it, Jean. I really will."

She settled for the safest response. "Don't disappoint him, Josh."

"I know. I get how important this is. And I won't disappoint him. I've got too much to make up for to mess this up. We'll figure it out." He stared into her eyes, again too close. "*We* will figure this out." His emphasis dug its way under her resistance like an undertow. For a breathtaking, terrifying moment, she thought he might kiss her—really kiss her, not just that careful peck on her cheek—and she couldn't be sure she would be able to fend him off. *I can't trust anything I'm feeling right now.*

Thankfully, Josh took her elbow instead. "So I'm not saying goodbye," he said with a soft insistence. "This is 'I'll see you soon,' got it?"

She nodded, her composure too fragile for words.

With a wave and a million-dollar smile, he turned from her and walked toward the terminal. In a matter of hours, he'd be back in his frantic California office, grabbing the world by the tail.

She stared after Josh as the glass doors slid closed behind him, pleading to Heaven that he wouldn't leave Jonah, and her, behind in his wake.

Chapter Eleven

Josh jabbed at the car stereo control button Monday morning, cranking it to the earsplitting volume he usually loved. He waited for the throbbing beat to course through him, underscoring the twisty drive to his office that launched his days.

The days he actually made it home from work, that was.

He couldn't remember the last time he'd been away from work for four days. Sales calls and conferences pulled him away from his desk frequently, but never to the level of disengagement of this past weekend. Half of him wondered what sort of disasters lay waiting on his desk, even though he'd been up for three hours poring over accumulated emails.

The other half of him—a half he didn't recognize—wanted to just keep driving. Take off down the highway in search of the quiet that had eluded him since the plane wheels touched down last night. He couldn't have stopped living loud; loud was who he was. His whole life was music and noise. It was about being loud and large, about being headed for greatness and impossible to ignore.

Josh Tyler was a high-volume guy in every respect.

So why did the noise just jar and annoy him this morning?

Chalking it up to jet lag, Josh applied the effort it took to make the left turn into SymphoCync's parking lot and told himself to enjoy the way the sun reflected off the building's huge glass windows. He had six meetings today, the first of which started in twenty minutes. As he hit the lock button on his key fob, making the car chirp out a sound from its "J. Tyler, CEO" parking spot, Josh made a small version of his name sign with his left hand. *Okay, Big Fish, time to hit the ground swimming.*

The day's meetings went by in an uninspiring blur. The next day's presentation went fine, but Josh felt no zing of success when the new advertisers signed their two-year contract.

On Wednesday Matt sent back a proposal Josh had given him to review with a dozen corrections. Mistakes Josh should have caught. "Get your head in the game" was scrawled across the bottom of the last page in Matt's all-caps handwriting.

On Thursday he snapped at his assistant for overbooking him in meetings. Overbooking. This from the guy for whom overbooking was usually standard operating mode.

Friday brought everything to a head, when Josh read an email from Hal Braddon, an important potential investor, about a deal they'd been working on for weeks. They were due to speak the next day at a weekend conference, but Braddon asked for a blisteringly early breakfast before the event began. At SymphoCync, not the hotel across town that was hosting the conference.

That was actually good news. Braddon was a high-profile investment capital magnate rich enough to buy tech companies for amusement if not for profit. The guy could say no any number of ways, or not respond at all. The fact that he wanted to meet privately told Josh the deal might be about to take a huge leap forward.

Josh slept in the office Friday night, working late and rising well before dawn to get ready for the monumental day ahead. It was still dark when the headlights of Hal Braddon's sleek convertible appeared in front of the building and Josh went down to meet him at the door.

Braddon was one of those guys who managed to make a tailored shirt and a pair of jeans look like a power suit. He never wore a suit because he never needed to—his powerful reputation and the size of his empire preceded him into any room. This morning, Tyler guessed there wasn't a single item of clothing or accessory on the man costing less than $200. Braddon's watch alone probably could have bought out Bill Williams's entire inventory. "I thought we'd go up to the rooftop terrace and watch the sun come up," Josh said as he shook Braddon's hand. "I've got coffee up there."

"Really good coffee, I hope?"

"Decent enough." The first rule in negotiations was to never look eager, to always look like you needed the deal less than the other guy. They rode the elevator up to the top floor just as the first pink streaks of sunrise were brightening the sky.

"Nice view," Braddon said as they walked out onto the terrace that overlooked the landscaped hillside. Even in the pale light of the arriving day, the scenery was breathtaking. The gorgeous view was one of the reasons Josh had bought the building, and certainly the reason he'd put in the garden patio.

"Keeps my head on straight," Josh replied. That wasn't a line; there had been chaotic weeks where ten minutes up here in the quiet was the only thing keeping a lid on his sanity.

"This can be a crazy business, but I love the pace. Do you?"

"Parts of it. I could do with more sleep than I'm getting. It helps that SymphoCync is packed with great people." It was. Personal music apps like SymphoCync weren't especially new ideas—it was the brilliant people Josh had gathered around him who'd taken a basic idea and made it sing. No other app had the sophistication of preference algorithms and the ease of use paired with the ability to surprise a customer with a "new favorite" like SymphoCync did. People gave him lots of the credit—and he worked harder than anyone else on staff—but it was the "symphony" of all the engineers, designers and technicians that made the success.

"Maybe," replied Braddon as he took the cup of coffee Josh offered. Normally Josh didn't handle refreshments, but with the exception of the overnight tech support staff, the building was empty. "I prefer to think it's the great leaders who make brilliance happen," Braddon went on. "Good tech is only half the battle—you know that." Braddon eased himself into one of the deck chairs with the grace of a man accustomed to having the upper hand in any room he entered. The fact that he could claim the upper hand, even on Josh's turf, spoke to the considerable power he wore with ease. "*I* know that."

"Takes a lot of capital to make brilliance keep happening, I know that," Josh replied as he sat down himself. Despite being only in his forties, Braddon already owned two media companies—one in video, the other in entertainment news—and had built up an empire. Josh had been pitching him for months to come in as a silent partner and wield that empire—and its very deep pockets—on SymphoCync's behalf.

"Well, I do believe we could do some pretty amazing things if we partner up." Braddon crossed one foot over the other knee, leaning back. Josh thought if the man had a cigar, he would have taken the time to light it at a leisurely pace.

Josh sipped his own coffee, knowing better than to fill the silence the man was laying out before him. This wasn't his first high-level negotiation. After a pause that felt entirely too long, Josh put down his cup and said, "You didn't ask for this meeting to tell me you're still thinking."

Braddon chuckled. "No."

So he had made a decision. Josh leaned in, ready to move things forward. "And a man like you doesn't come clear across town before dawn to pass on a deal." Anticipation buzzed like an electric current under his skin.

"I pick the people I do business with very carefully." He leveled Josh with a fierce, unflinching look. "You and I, though, we're cut from the same cloth. Strong ideas. Bold moves. We're risk takers. I like you. I've already told you I want to work with you." After a pause he repeated, "You. I do deals with people, not companies."

How much longer were they going to dance around Braddon's response? "Fair enough."

After drinking his coffee to a remarkably unnerving dramatic effect, Braddon declared, "I'm here to make a counteroffer. I don't want a silent partnership. I want to buy SymphoCync outright. For an obscene amount of money. You'll never have to mess around with public offerings or venture capital, and I'll probably approve whatever executive structure you want. But only in a full buyout."

Josh took pains to hide his surprise. Sell SymphoCync? Could he really go that far, even if it got him what the company needed?

"I meant what I said—I back people, not companies. I'm backing you," Braddon explained, "but I'll back you as owner, not investor. That's the offer I came 'clear across town,' as you say, to make."

I wouldn't own SymphoCync. The thought seemed impossible. Taking on Hal Braddon as a partner, a backer, was one thing. Reporting to him as boss? That was quite another.

"I get that you're not a 'work for someone else' kind of guy," Braddon continued. "And I know selling SymphoCync isn't what we talked about. But I've decided it's what I want. And I'm used to paying for what I want. Handsomely." With that, Braddon pulled a single sheet of paper from the sleek leather portfolio he carried and spread it out on the table between them.

Josh stared at the number. For a drawn-out second, his mind went a thousand directions with what Braddon's $240 million—*million*—could do.

"I'm about to make SymphoCync a legend, Tyler," Braddon went on. "Think about it—with that kind of capital, there won't be another company that can touch your market share."

"*Your* market share," Josh countered.

"Now don't get petty. It'll be *our* market share," Braddon returned. "You retain full autonomy. It'll still be your company in all the ways that matter. You still run the show."

Josh heard his father's voice: *never forget, son, it's the man who has the money who makes the rules.* "What's to say you don't turn around and fire me the day after you take ownership?"

"I wouldn't. As a matter of fact, I'm going to stipulate you stay on as CEO for four years minimum. I have no interest in running SymphoCync."

"Just in *owning* it," Josh shot back. Here he thought he'd landed the perfect deal to add assets for the growth SymphoCync needed, and he'd been outmaneuvered. He'd considered himself above a buyout. Even a multimillion-dollar one like this.

"Really, this can't come as a total surprise," Braddon said as he stood up.

Shame on me, Josh thought. "Let's just say you're living up to your reputation."

Braddon laughed. "Good to hear. So now you've got my terms. You and I have a conference to attend in—" he checked the fancy watch "—two hours, so you know where to find me when you have an answer." With that, Braddon headed off the terrace, but stopped for a moment to turn back. "You'll still be the man who made SymphoCync, Josh. I'm not taking that away from you."

Josh had a dozen responses brewing in his head, but the set of Braddon's spine told Josh the man had said what he came to say. Any arguments would fall on deaf ears.

Deaf ears. He was going to have to stop thinking stuff like that.

He watched Braddon's silhouette disappear through the door and be swallowed up in the gorgeous reflection of the sunshine that now bounced off the glass. How had this become the month of people setting off bombs in his life?

He had to reject Braddon's arrogant offer. Didn't he? He was Josh Tyler—he was the boss, the innovator—and SymphoCync was his.

Run, not *own*? The thought choked him. It was a dizzying amount of money. Jonah would need therapies and schooling and college and doctors...

The impossible contradiction that was his future had just managed to become twice as impossible.

Chapter Twelve

Jean sat at the kitchen table going over tomorrow's schedule while she waited for the water to boil. Tomorrow's bus excursion for the dozen Asheville wedding planners could be a major step forward for Matrimony Valley. Especially if *North Carolina Nuptials* magazine sent a photographer like they promised. It had been a flurry of work to send out all those press releases and email invitations on top of the final preparations for Violet's wedding over Memorial Day weekend, but if even one of the twelve booked a wedding in the valley, the effort would pay for itself. Plus, affairs that already came with wedding planners in tow made her job that much easier.

She had Josh to thank for that particular idea—marketing to planners as well as to brides. It would feel good to let him know how well it had worked out.

If he called, that was.

She looked up from her papers to see Jonah playing with the tablet Josh had sent to him. Josh had never actually promised to video chat every day, but when he'd done so for the first three days, Jonah had come to expect it. That's how little boys' minds worked. All Jonah knew was that Big Fish hadn't called in four days. He didn't understand that his new friend Big Fish had a huge company to run.

Quite frankly, the connection between those two frightened her. The way Jonah looked at Josh, Jean could almost believe her son could somehow recognize his father. As if their DNA called to each other in a way only Jonah's deaf ears could hear.

"What are you drawing?" she signed, nodding toward the digital illustration program Jonah had recently discovered. She'd found him bent over the tablet more often than not recently, his small pink tongue stuck out in serious concentration as his finger swiped over the surface.

She hardly needed to ask; Jonah drew the same thing over and over. Fish. Almost always in heartbreaking pairs of big fish and little fish, occasionally in startling family trios—a big, a medium and a small fish. He never named them, never said who the fish were, just drew fish. Was he sending her a deliberate message? Was his small brain working through whatever he'd picked up on between her and Josh? Or was he just a boy expressing his fascination for finned creatures?

Don't you dare leave him hanging. Jean sent her silent plea to Josh across the miles. *Don't make me glad I held off letting him know who you are.*

She hadn't meant to turn this week into some sort of test, some unintentional hurdle Josh must jump to earn the right to call himself Jonah's father. She'd never asked him for daily communication with Jonah or herself. She'd intentionally stayed away from making any demands on him at all. No, it was Josh's own enthusiastic promises that had ignited all these dangerous hopes that now clanged around in her chest. Everything Josh did—or didn't do—seemed heavy with too much meaning right now. She read and reread his few emails, the handful of text messages and photos, dissecting them for clues to his intentions. She scoured his expressions on the three days he did video chat with Jonah, searching for signs of waning attention. She couldn't stop herself from jumping to conclusions, from waiting for things to go wrong, to fall apart. After all, hadn't life shown her how easily things fell apart?

All this casual-appearing vigilance was exhausting. Pretending this very big deal was no big deal was sapping energy that she should be using elsewhere.

Like on the twelve wedding planners who needed to be impressed tomorrow.

Back in college, there had been a final she'd botched because Josh had made some wild, eloquent promise of a celebration. He'd painted such a fantastic picture of how he was going to take her on a picnic inside the campus telescope silo, showing her stars and promising her the moon, that she'd been too distracted to do well on the crucial test. His ability to persuade her, to distract her to the point of derailing, had flustered her that day. It made her feel weak and impressionable. All those feelings were replaced with anger when he didn't show at the silo at the appointed time. The scene had replayed dozens of times while they were in San Jose.

He'd had a good excuse that night. Something about a professor and a lab lockdown or whatever. That was the hard thing about Josh—he always had a good excuse. Loads of them. Only good excuses could pile up with as much weight as poor ones. She'd lost count of the number of times she'd found herself alone at a restaurant, coffee shop or her own dining room table. She never seemed to matter as much as whatever crisis arose—and the crises always arose. Jean wanted to matter, even if only to one person. It's what made it easy to come home to the faithfulness of her father, to the valley, where it felt like she mattered a great deal.

The water boiled, the spaghetti cooked and Jonah talked about fish during his bath. She pulled the tablet from his hands as his eyes fell closed in sleep, wanting to call Josh and yell at him.

You can't have his heart. Or mine. Not if we're going to be on the sidelines like this.

As she placed it on the nightstand, the notification light illuminated with a quiet ping. Opening it up, she found a message from Josh. It was just like him to come in under the wire, to save himself at the last possible moment.

A photo appeared in the message feed. A goofy selfie, a shot of himself smiling and pointing to the front of an expensive-looking refrigerator. Jonah's drawing was fixed to the door by a set of four shiny magnets. Newly purchased, she somehow knew, for the purpose.

That was the thing about Josh—he was the kind of man she could never quite hate. He could irritate the living daylights out of her, push her to the limits of her grace and patience, and then somehow manage to save himself with a grand gesture, a perfectly phrased apology or just the right plea. It was what made him professionally great…and personally impossible.

It was why she kept him out of her life. She could

never seem to put limits on how he invaded her good sense. Some part of her could only do "all or nothing" when it came to Josh Tyler.

And now neither one was a viable choice.

Jean sighed, closed the tablet and put it down. She snapped off the light in Jonah's room and walked to the kitchen table, where her files and her cell phone lay. After a brief prayer for wisdom, she tapped the contact on her phone for Josh and pressed Dial.

"Hey there" came Josh's energetic voice over the line. "Did he like my shot?"

"He's asleep. It's eight thirty here."

"Oh, yeah. It's earlier here. I haven't even thought about dinner."

Another way their lives were vastly different. "But you're home. That's unusual for you, isn't it?"

"I had to get out of the office tonight. I…um… I had some thinking to do."

That was curious. "About what?" She wasn't altogether sure she wanted to hear the answer.

His sigh was weary. "Not now."

She didn't know what to say to that. Was it a work worry, or was he pondering how to mesh their lives for Jonah's sake? Every way to ask the question seemed loaded with pressure. She settled for "Sorry."

"Don't be." After a bit of a pause where she thought she was going to just have to end with "Good night," he said, "I've decided I'm going to come back and stay through Violet's wedding."

That startled her. "Really?"

"Yeah. You know, take a bite out of those fifty-some-odd vacation days I have piled up."

The Josh she'd known would have vacationed—if he vacationed at all—someplace exotic, remote and expensive. Matrimony Valley, even for Violet's wedding, didn't seem to fit the bill.

"Why?" Jean tried to make the question sound supportive, curious, instead of a question of motive. She was fishing for some declaration of wanting to spend time with Jonah, she knew that, but couldn't seem to help herself.

He sighed again—something that seemed odd, even for the new Josh—before answering. "I can't seem to think here."

She didn't know what to make of that answer, or the disjointed way he gave it. "Meaning?"

"I have to make a big decision—a business one, I mean—and I can't seem to get my head in the right place to make it out here. I did an important conference this weekend. I love those things—or I used to. This last one just felt too loud and frantic all of a sudden."

Loud and frantic was Josh's native habitat—or had been. Certainly more than sleepy, slow-paced Matrimony Valley.

"You're welcome here. I'm sure Violet will love to have you serve as her advance team." *Go on, say it.* "Jonah will be happy, too."

"I want to tell him, Jean. I want him to know."

She closed her eyes, feeling the power of his demand even across the miles. "He will know. We just have to go slowly here. You've got to be ready to be who he needs you to be." She recalled the sight of Jonah's eager little eyes. He'd latched on to Josh already somehow. Did she really have the right to delay his knowing any longer? At five, did he have the capacity to understand a situation this complicated? "Big Fish not calling for days is different—really different—from Daddy not calling for days. Than Daddy not being here."

"I'm coming. I just told you I'm coming."

Frustration knotted her stomach. "You told me you were coming to think, not coming to see Jonah."

"Of course I'm coming to see Jonah. Why would I have to say that?" She heard him blow out a breath with all the frustration she felt. "What is it you want from me, Jean?"

What is it you want from me?

That was a dumb question to ask Jean. He knew exactly what Jean wanted from him. She'd never come out and demanded it—just as she'd never expressed her true needs when they were together—but at least this time he knew what she wanted. What she needed. Jonah's father had to be all-in, or not in at all.

All-in. Suddenly *everyone* wanted "all-in" from him. It shouldn't irritate him; complete commitment had been his style for years. The Murphy bed that pulled down from the wall of his office and the barely lived-in state of his apartment offered evidence of that. Hadn't each of the few women he'd dated since Jean said the same thing? "Expensive gifts aren't attention" the most recent one had shouted at him as she tossed a costly bracelet down on his desk—his desk because he hadn't shown up at the restaurant for their dinner reservation—two months ago. He'd gone "all-in" on lots of things, but never with the people in his life. And where had that gotten him?

And now, Hal Braddon wouldn't put his money behind SymphoCync unless he got to buy the firm, and without Josh contractually declaring himself "all-in" for the next four years. Turning down Braddon's offer would be denying the best opportunity for growth SymphoCync had, hobbling the company and the dozens of people who had given their "all-in" to get it this far.

How was he supposed to be two different Joshes on two different coasts? "No either, no neither," as his father was fond of classifying impossible choices.

Jean's silence on the other end of the line told him they were verging on an argument he didn't want to have. "I'm still figuring out how to do this. Aren't you?"

"Yes." Her voice was quiet.

He leaned against the fridge, one finger running down the waxy crayon of Jonah's drawing. He wanted to be all-in for Jonah—foreign as that desire was given his own history. It felt beyond frustrating to be denied it, even if he could see Jean had that right. "So I don't see why I can't figure it out as Jonah's father."

"Because fathers are forever to someone his age." It was all there in how she said the word; she doubted he had *forever* in him. Wow, that stung.

And rightly so; he doubted he had it in himself. But he really, really wanted the chance to try.

"We can make this work." He knew the insistence was rising in his voice, but he couldn't seem to help it.

"How?"

"I don't know that yet." *I had an idea how to make this work before Hal Braddon decided to start giving ultimatums.* That still threw him—ultimatums were Dad's weapon of choice, not his. Two weeks ago the concept of being legally bound to SymphoCync—his technical baby—for the next four years would have been a no-brainer. Braddon was his professional idol, Josh's first choice for the man to finance Sympho-Cync's launch to the next level. Now his world strained to hold Jonah and SymphoCync at the same time. And this pull back to the valley? Josh was at a total loss for how to handle that.

That sleepy little town wasn't his world. This was. So why couldn't he sleep? Why couldn't he think? Why did the long hours suddenly seem like a burden and Braddon's price of commitment so high?

Jean's sigh on the other end of the line brought him back to the moment. "I know I haven't called. That's exactly why I want to come back again. I want to see him." Before he even recognized it in himself, he heard the words "I want to see you" leave his mouth with the startling surprise of truth. He did want to see her again. Very much. The strong, tenacious woman she'd become fascinated him. She seemed so centered, so grounded, despite the huge risk she'd undertaken with Matrimony Valley.

He, on the other hand, felt like he was living in a pinball machine, wildly bouncing from one force to another, racking up points that did nothing but rank him on some list that never really mattered. "I need to figure something out, and I want to figure it out with you."

He imagined Matt rolling his eyes at the gooey nature of his words. He normally worked out company tactics like this with Matt. Any problem, actually— Matt was his sounding board for all things personal and professional. But Josh hadn't even told Matt about Braddon's counteroffer of purchase. He told himself it was because information like that ignited rumors in a heartbeat, but that wasn't the entire reason. He hadn't told anyone about any of this.

Part of it was how Braddon's "no you, no deal" insistence made him feel oddly and uncomfortably indispensable. That was weird in itself, seeing how he'd built his career to be exactly that: synonymous with Sympho-Cync. He should want SymphoCync to need him. He should be dying to stay, excited to keep on. The eighty-two people who worked at SymphoCync needed him to stay on, because growing at a spectacular pace was the only way anyone stayed alive in the hyperspeed world of technology. In this world, you paused, you died.

"What are you saying, Josh? What are you looking for?"

A pause. The words pinned him to the wall. He wanted to hit the pause button on the rocket ride that had been his life since school, and that was all kinds of wrong.

Wasn't it?

"Can I come back now?" It was a ridiculous question. He didn't need permission to hop a plane back to Matrimony Valley. He was obligated to return there in less than a week as it was, given Violet's impending wedding. His question wasn't really about location, though; it was about proximity to Jean and to Jonah. He wanted to figure out why she invaded his thoughts. He wanted to know if the pull he felt toward her was nostalgia or something different. Something new, something he'd been missing for too long. None of it made sense except the weird notion that it made even less sense here than there.

Silence dragged between them. Her hesitation pressed against him.

"Be careful, Josh."

Careful? He'd never been careful, ever. He'd bush-whacked his way through life, cutting down resistance in front of him with little regard to what fell in the process. It struck him, as he mulled over the warning in her voice, that he didn't really know how to be careful.

Jean knew that. Even before he knew it, she'd recognized the damage he might do. Not out of spite or malice, but out of sheer blunt force and power. "Can I come back now?" he asked again, astonished to hear pleading in his voice.

Her answer told him a lot about the both of them. "I can't stop you."

"I'm asking, Jean. Not telling, asking." She had to know what strange territory that was for him, didn't she?

There was a long pause before she said, "Yes."

He sank against the refrigerator in an unexpected feeling of relief. For a man who was used to moving mountains to get what he wanted, the art of the request was a foreign language. This new, weird world where "apply more force, skill or money" wasn't the path to a solution was going to take a lot of getting used to.

"Thank you," he said softly.

"Be careful," she said again. The fact that she had to repeat it punctured whatever confidence he had left. *Could* he do this? Get to know his son, and Jean, in a way that added to their lives instead of just complicating them?

He gave the only answer he could, and one that rang insufficient in his ears for hours after he hung up: "I promise you, Jean, I will try."

Chapter Thirteen

Matt looked predictably stunned after Josh gave him the entire explanation as they sat on the rooftop deck that evening. "You can't leave. You just got back."

"I was already taking time off for Vi's wedding. Just think of this as adding on a bit more."

"It's not like that at all," Matt countered.

"Well…" That was the best and the worst thing about Matt. He never let Josh get away with anything.

Matt ran his hands through his hair. "You sure this isn't some kind of wunderkind-is-about-to-turn-thirty identity crisis?"

"I don't think so."

"You said you'd never sell SymphoCync. I mean, you *are* SymphoCync. You've always been SymphoCync."

Matt began pacing the deck, his brain already starting the calculations that made him so valuable to the company. "That's some serious cash. You've been chasing Braddon for months, and now you've got him. I don't like the sale part, granted, but if he's saying it

really will be hands-off and you'll still be at the helm,
I think we can live with that—provided the contract's
airtight."

"I know," Josh agreed.

"You know what that kind of cash can do for us."
Matt began pacing faster. "Get legal on it, lock down
your position and authority, draw lines around his, and
we can make it work."

"I know," Josh repeated.

Matt stopped and looked at Josh. "We can launch
the video platform with that kind of capital. It'll mean
we'll be running flat out for a few more years, but we
know how to do that. We do that better than anybody."

The thought of "running flat out" for a few more
years soured Josh's stomach. *I used to be the flat-out-
give-150-percent king. Now I want to go fishing. What's
happening to me?*

Matt walked toward him. "This isn't just about SymphoCync and whether or not you're ready to sell, is it."
He didn't phrase it like a question. "Look, I know this
whole Jean-and-the-kid thing is weighing on you." It
struck Josh that while Matt had been pacing the deck
furiously for the whole conversation, Josh hadn't moved
from his seat. "You can figure out how to be in his life.
From here," Matt urged. "There are ways to make this
work. Jean's obviously figured out how to make it work
without you, so anything you bring to the table's just
an improvement, right?"

When Josh didn't answer, Matt went on. "I mean,
when you do this deal, you'll have enough money to
give that kid whatever he needs and then some. He'll
have access to anything, thanks to you."

But he won't have access to what he needs most of all—me. After all, wasn't it true that his own father had access to endless resources and had never given him what he truly needed? The dual forces tearing at Josh seemed to rip him right down his spine. "I want to be a father, not just a support check."

"Okay, so let's figure out how to do that."

"I can't figure it out here!" Josh shouted, his frustration boiling over. "I can't…think here. Not right now."

"What? Suddenly now your brilliance doesn't work on this coast?" Matt threw up his hands. "What's gotten into you? You're letting this derail you, and derail maybe the biggest deal of your career."

"I know the timing's lousy, but I need to go. I know you don't understand why, but that doesn't change that I need to go."

Matt started for the door. "Fine. Go. Go hang out in your mountains and get whatever this is out of your system so you can come back and make this work. I'll cover for you. I can't believe I'm saying that, but maybe it's something I'm going to have to get used to, isn't it?"

"Matt…"

Matt jabbed a finger at him. "Don't. Don't even try. Let's just hope Braddon's offer didn't come with an expiration date. 'Cause he doesn't strike me as the kind of man who's going to sit around and wait for you to wrestle with your conscience." With that, Josh watched his partner and friend of eight years stomp off down the hall.

The mountains. Jean knew there were mountains in other parts of the country—other parts of the world, for that matter—but her mountains never ceased to amaze her. To soothe her and grant her the perspective that so easily slid from her life. Did city people realize how much they didn't see? Did people in plains states know how many shades of purple could outline the mountains as they spread out before you in the afternoon? How they changed and shifted like an ocean as the sun sank?

Josh pulled in a deep breath beside her. He'd looked wound up and exhausted when he came into town this morning. The distance that had been their undoing seemed to loom again. Neither of them ever reached out when they ought to have, and she feared those old mistakes would doom this new relationship, whatever it was becoming. There was so much still unresolved. Josh hadn't spoken of what had happened in California, even though she could see it weighed on him.

So she did what she always did when things weighed on her. She took him up into the mountains while Jonah had a playdate with Lulu at Kelly's. If they were going to make their way to a solution, here was the place where it could most easily happen.

It hadn't started out easy. They'd been sitting for almost an hour in silence until Jean felt the stress slowly slough off both of them. She wanted to let him be the first to open up.

"I used to think," he said finally, "that 'purple mountain majesties' was just a song lyric."

She laughed, glad to hear the vista had the same effect on him that it did on her "You have mountains in California. You have cliffs and crashing seas. And I'm sure there are loads more song lyrics about the California coast than about the Smoky Mountains. I mean, just the Beach Boys alone…"

"Well, yeah, but I didn't expect this. I mean, I remember how you used to talk about this place, but I didn't expect it to…to stick to me like this. The peace of it all. The place is thick with peace, you know that?"

Peace. Isn't that what they both needed? Peace over their past and peace about how they'd craft their future? She gave him a smile. "And what's California thick with?"

"Smog. Ambition. Drama."

"Oh, we've got drama here. One town council meeting here could take on a month of West Coast power lunches, I assure you."

He pounded one fist on his forehead, as if he could shake the right words loose. He was wrestling with something huge. "It's not the same. That place is thick with…whatever the opposite of this place is."

She knew what he was trying to say. What he was trying to articulate was much of the reason she was here and not there. Still, she understood his grasp for the words, seeing as she'd never really found a suitable way to explain it herself. "But you love it there, don't you?"

He didn't answer, just let out a groan of frustration. The wonderful and terrifying thought that he might be catching the affection for the valley—the affinity that ran through her veins—hitched her breath.

Close the distance. Don't make the old mistakes, she told herself. "Josh, what's going on? Why are you here, now, looking like you do?"

He leaned back against the tree, the weariness seeming to double in his eyes, as if he suddenly needed the ancient trunk to hold him upright. "Hal Braddon."

"Who's he?"

That made him laugh. "The fact that you have to ask just underscores the whole thing."

That had been one of the things that grew the distance between them—he would make a problem sound like it was above her ability to help. She wasn't going to let that happen anymore. "I never liked it when you were condescending, Josh."

He sat upright, his elbow on one knee. "Sorry. That's not how I meant it."

"So explain it to me."

He shifted to face her. "Everybody in my business knows Hal Braddon. If I'm a big fish, Braddon's a whale. Everybody knows what that man can do."

"Which is…?"

"That whale can throw his very considerable capital behind businesses so that they take off into the stratosphere. Everybody in my corner of the world wants Hal to get behind their business. It's pretty much the golden ticket. I've been courting the guy for two years. He finally came through earlier this week. Made me a very pretty offer." He looped his finger in the air. "Lots and lots of digits that could do lots and lots of things for SymphoCync."

She could understand that. What she couldn't understand was the lack of victory in his eyes. "That's what you always wanted, isn't it? Build a big company? Be the legend who launched SymphoCync?"

He slumped back against the tree. "Hal exceeded all

expectations, I'll give him that much. His offer is a full thirty percent above what I was hoping for."

Jean pulled her knees up to hug them. "So? I don't get it."

"Hal doesn't want to *back* my company, he wants to *buy* it. He wants to own SymphoCync."

"Are you interested in selling?" she asked as carefully as she could. Selling SymphoCync would enable Josh to start over anywhere in the world. Including someplace far closer to here.

"Braddon's big funding comes with a high price tag. One that's become a bit higher than I was expecting."

"Help me understand." She paused, then made herself ask, "Does it have to do with me and Jonah? Is that why you're here?" She hadn't expected to be so frightened of the answer.

"Selling to Braddon will double SymphoCync's assets, but only if I sign a four-year contract to stay on as CEO." Only Josh Tyler could give a look that could throw a woman off balance when she was already sitting on the ground. "Under any other circumstances, the ink would already be dry on an offer like that. It's a dream setup."

"But?"

He held her gaze. "But I'd be running full tilt in San Jose for the next four years if I sign."

"And?" The whole mountainside held its breath alongside her.

"And that will cost me."

He'd found the exact knife edge between realization and decision, hadn't he? On the one hand, her prayers had been answered—Josh had realized the value of his son and the role he could have as Jonah's father. On the other hand, he stood at the apex of her greatest fear—that he would still choose something else over that role. It was their whole relationship—and their biggest issue—wrapped up in five words.

"I've been thinking a lot since Braddon made that offer. About what I want, and what I'm willing to pay to get it. And, I suppose, what's worthwhile."

"Those are big questions." Certainly ones that had weighed on her in recent days.

"I'm sorry for what happened to our relationship. It's more than the collateral damage of a dynamic career, although I'm sure that's how Dad would have put it."

"True," she admitted. She certainly felt like Bartholomew Tyler viewed her and Jonah as expendable complications.

Josh looked into her eyes. "It's my fault. I ignored you. I took your love and loyalty for granted. I gave you reasons to leave and reasons to think you couldn't come to me with Jonah. I'm not expecting you to forgive me just because life's thrown us back together."

He looked away for a minute, as if he were uncharacteristically gathering courage for whatever he would say next. Jean felt her heart do a flip in her chest. "Braddon's offer feels like it might cost me everything. Like it would cost me what it would take to earn your forgiveness and my place in Jonah's life."

Yes, her heart seemed to chime with the truth of his words and how much she'd needed to hear them. *He really is coming to understand.*

"That's why I can't figure out what to do. That's why I'm here."

"But we're talking about it, talking through it," she offered. "I never gave you that chance. I took that chance away by leaving because it felt easier. I wouldn't have to see my fault in things if I put all the blame on you." She said what felt like the most important thing of all. "We're going to both need to forgive each other if we stand any chance at all."

That brought his eyes up to burn into hers. "Do you want us to have a chance?"

She held his gaze, even though it seemed to hollow out her chest to do so. "A you-and-I 'us', not just a Jonah's parents 'us'?"

He reached for her hand. "I don't think I want to walk away from this a second time. I can't ignore that the world's given us another chance at this."

"God's given us another chance at this," she corrected. No matter what she was starting to feel, no matter how the thought of redeeming their history tugged at her heartstrings, Jean didn't want to build a life with a man whose own life couldn't include the faith that held her and Jonah together.

She waited for him to pull his hand away at her correction, but he didn't. Instead, he intertwined his fingers with hers. "You know, I'm surprised by how easily I can think that. Here, that is."

She looked at their joined hands. "God isn't only in North Carolina, Josh."

"Let's not make the same mistakes as last time. Let's work this out together, you and me." He closed his eyes for a second. "Only it's not just about you and me, is it?"

"You mean Jonah?"

"Jonah, too, but it's even bigger than that, Jean. Those eighty-two people who work at SymphoCync—it's their careers on the line, too. I walk away from this deal with Braddon, and they'll feel it as well as me. It'll take me years to put together another deal this good, and in that time we could slow our growth—which is as good as death in my world. You don't just waltz away from an offer like Hal Braddon's."

They'd never talked over issues like this back in California. He'd never really let her into his world. "You make him sound like a mafia boss. There's no such thing as 'a deal you can't refuse'—is there?"

Josh shook his head with a dark laugh that let her know that's just how he saw it—emotionally if not logically. "Not like that. But those people—the ones who work at SymphoCync—they put in long hours, too. They've made lots of sacrifices to get us where we are now. I can't just suddenly decide it's okay to be here and let them down." He gazed at her. "Any more than you can decide it's okay to let the valley down." After a long moment, he said, "We can't ignore that people depend on us."

She knew at that moment that he did indeed feel what she felt—a rekindling of the feelings that had brought Jonah into the world in the first place. Only this time it wasn't so one-sided. It wasn't just her riding the tail of his brilliant comet—there was an equality to them that had never been there before.

And now that equality might be the very thing to keep them apart. They'd each succeeded. Separately. Which meant he had a vast enterprise bent on tugging him away from her while she had roots and dreams binding her here.

Yes, he was here now, and they were finally dealing with the things that had damaged their relationship earlier. But he couldn't change who he was any more than she could change who she was. Hal Braddon's offer shackled him to SymphoCync. She could see now that he'd try hard to find some way to be in both worlds, but it wasn't really possible. Even if it worked for a short while, it would never last. Not for what Jonah would need or what she knew her own heart would want.

"People do depend on us," she said, feeling her heart gain a sharp, deep crack, "and maybe that's why we can't always have what we want."

Chapter Fourteen

❧

The next morning was filled with wedding business tasks—making follow-up phone calls to the Asheville wedding planners who had expressed an interest, ordering direction signs to be placed out for Violet's guests, and solving an argument between the church and the inn over where to keep the rented chairs before they were set out the morning of the ceremony.

Josh had requested Jean stop by the inn before picking Jonah up from school. When she met him in the front parlor, he was holding a small black box. "There were a dozen other projects I was supposed to be working on back in San Jose," he said, "but I couldn't stop working on this." Lifting the lid, Josh produced something that looked similar to Jonah's handheld gaming device: a little larger than a smartphone, with chunky grips on each side suitable for little hands. It had a large screen. It didn't look mass-produced. Instead, it looked like something Josh had made himself.

"Why did you wait until now?" she wondered aloud.

He'd made no mention of this last night, and he had always been impatient to share new toys or gadgets.

"It wasn't quite perfect. And…" He paused for a moment before lowering his voice to say, "…I wanted yesterday to be about you and me."

That skittered down her spine. "What is it?" she asked, just to keep the conversation on safer ground.

He held it up and pointed to the label that read Jonahphone. When she raised an eyebrow, he held it closer and said, "I fabricated this just for Jonah. There isn't another like it in the world."

Jean's heart both warmed and pinched at his efforts. "Jonah can't really use a cell phone, Josh. He can't hear, and he can't read enough to text." Not that those facts had stopped Josh when he *did* take the time to communicate with Jonah. In fact, Josh and Jonah had somehow managed to have amusing—if cryptic— "conversations" totally in emoji over the tablet he'd given her son earlier.

"I know that," replied Josh. "This isn't that kind of phone. It's more like the gramophone kind. It's for music."

That sounded like an even worse idea. "Music?"

"Watch." Josh took the device and turned it on. "I've set it to my SymphoCync account and the Wi-Fi here at the inn, but I can show you how to set up your own account and link it to the network at your house. Or download songs so Jonah can play them anywhere."

Jean wasn't sure how to respond to this attempt to drag Jonah into Josh's world of music. It wasn't really possible—not in any way that made a difference. Then again, Josh Taylor was always the kind of man to take "impossible" as a challenge rather than a barrier. Maybe he really was capable of breaking down Jonah's personal "sound barrier" when it came to music.

"You still love 'Obladi Oblada'?" Josh asked.

She'd always loved Beatles tunes—still did. The first night she realized she was in love with Josh, they had danced in her dorm room to "Something." Josh had sung it in her ear, sending tingles down her spine. For a man who made his career in music, he couldn't carry a tune in a bucket, but that charmed her all the more.

"Sure," she replied, rather unsure of where this was going.

Josh tapped his way through a simple menu of icons that appeared on the screen, selecting the song title from a short list. "And Jonah's favorite color is green, right?"

She allowed herself a small surge of admiration that he remembered. "It is."

Josh tapped a few more times on the screen, then handed her the device. "Hold it on either side, where the grips are."

She followed his instructions, watching as an animated countdown flashed "3…2…1," and then the device launched into action. The music came from the speakers, yes, but so many other things happened. The notes buzzed in her palms—high and light or low and harder, alternating between grips, wondrously letting her hands "feel" the music. At the same time, amazing shifting shapes that somehow managed to mimic the song bounced across the screen. She was experiencing the song—its rhythm, its volume, even somehow the flow of the lyrics—in multiple ways other than just sound. It was nothing short of astounding.

"It's music for Jonah. The program will take any song and transform it into sensation and visuals. Later, when he can read, I can upgrade it to show lyrics, but he won't need that for a while, I guess."

The intensity of his eyes and the brilliance of his "I made this" grin made it hard to breathe. She'd had Jonah put his hands up to stereo speakers or let him watch the soundboard readouts at a radio station, but nothing came close to what she now held. "Josh, it's… amazing."

"I couldn't stand the idea of not being able to share SymphoCync or music with Jonah. I kept thinking there had to be a way. So I just kept fiddling until I came up with this. If you knew how behind I was on a ton of projects because I couldn't seem to stop building this…"

Jean wanted to throw her arms around his neck and kiss him for what he'd done. It stunned her how easily she could slide back into that person, that woman who watched Josh Tyler take on the world and win. He'd taken that genius and wielded it, unrelentingly, on behalf of her son.

On behalf of *his* son.

For a fragile moment, she could feel both of them teetering on the brink of going back there. To being those people, those two hearts joined as one. It hummed between them as fiercely as if it were playing out of the Jonahphone.

"Can I show it to him?" Josh finally said, looking all too much like a kid eager to play with his own toy—or in this case, let his son play with the toy he'd invented. "I felt like I ought to ask you first."

The Josh she'd known rarely asked anyone for permission to do anything. He'd always been a "do first, get clearance later" kind of man. Had he really changed? Or had she come off as that fiercely protective where Jonah was concerned?

The smile she gave him radiated up from a grateful heart. "I think he'll love it. Let's go show him now."

His smile widened. "I was hoping you'd say that."

Josh's heart couldn't seem to decide if it was pounding or swelling. Probably both. His job lately involved so many hours staring at spreadsheets and readouts that he'd forgotten the sheer joy of making something. Of inventing and creating. It was hard to beat the unique zing of putting something into the world that wasn't there before.

But to be inventing and creating a way for his own son to hear the music that formed his world? Well, that was a whole new kind of zing that made everything else on his desk—everything else in the world, truthfully—look tedious. He'd made million-dollar presentations and not been as excited—and anxious— as he was as they stood outside Jonah's school.

Jean picked up on his tension, and touched his hand that held the box he'd shown her earlier. "He'll love it. It's wonderful." Those impossibly blue eyes of hers always could speak calm to him in ways even Matt had never achieved. Matt calmed him with facts and tactics—and that was useful—but Jean could calm him just by *being Jean*.

How had he not realized how much he missed that? How had he not noticed how he hadn't been calm for years? The constant frantic pace of his life he'd come to think of as normal wasn't supposed to *be* normal. There was another way to live. Oh, sure, he could construct some semblance of a slower life in California, but it would be lacking Jean and Jonah. So it would never feel whole. It sounded stupid to his practical nature, but making this device for Jonah made him feel whole. It closed some circle in his life he hadn't even realized was left hanging open.

A woman walked Jonah out of the school, signing at a rapid rate with him. "That's his teacher with the deaf sister, Gina. Gina signs very well, but we also get an interpreter in to help two days a week. We're hoping it will be five when he starts first grade. Gina's such a blessing—we'd have to go to a school forty minutes away without her."

Josh watched Gina's fingers fly, wondering if he'd ever get to that level of proficiency.

He would. He'd put in the effort, find the time. Jonah was worth it.

"A great day, Jean," Gina said while signing. "Smart kid you've got here." Watching Jonah wave, Gina asked Jonah, "Who's this?"

Josh felt Jean tense beside him—when was it going to be easier to answer that question?

"My friend Big Fish," Jonah signed. The sign for friend both pleased and irritated Josh. He was ready to be more than a friend to his son. Still, that timetable was Jean's to decide. If he was honest with himself, he hoped today's gift would move things along in that direction, would help to demonstrate whatever commitment Jean needed to see to be ready to tell Jonah who he really was.

Gina laughed at the unusual name. "Hello, Big Fish," she said while signing the greeting. Jean had explained that Jonah used "signed English" because of his place in a hearing world. American Sign Language, what Jonah would eventually use as he became older, was a completely different language. There were so many hurdles to this. Maybe that's why the Jonahphone felt like such an important first step.

"Miss Gina, this is Josh Tyler," Jean said, hesitating just a moment before adding, "a friend of the family."

A friend of the family. It was better than "an ex from California," but not by enough.

"See you tomorrow, sport," Gina said, signing "goodbye" and heading back toward the school.

"Big Fish brought something for you," Jean said and signed, nodding toward a bench a short ways away. "Something really special."

Jonah's eyes lit up in the way any kid's would with the promise of a present. He stared at the box as they walked toward the bench. Josh loved how Jonah sat down right next to him, practically climbing on his lap in eagerness. He caught Jean's eye, feeling the communication gap loom large again. "I'm gonna need your help here. I don't know the right signs to explain it."

He went through the same short explanation he'd given Jean, but in terms Jonah could understand, about wanting to share his music in a way fit for Jonah and about how he built it, delighted at Jonah's giggle at the name Jonahphone.

"Will it work out here? There's no Wi-Fi," Jean whispered as Josh showed Jonah how to turn it on.

"I downloaded 'Obladi Oblada' so it'll play anywhere. We can add songs he likes later." Did Jonah have songs he liked? Could he? He would, if the device worked the way Josh hoped it would.

Josh's pulse seemed to thud in his ears as he positioned Jonah's hands over the grips. They fit perfectly—he'd made it just the right size. He didn't even have to tell Jonah to push the large green circle that appeared on the screen. When the animated countdown began, Jonah squealed with anticipation—a sound that rang through Josh's chest.

Jonah's eyes popped wide as the song began to play and send vibrations to his palms. He laughed as the shapes and forms flowed across the screen in green and other colors. When his head began to nod in time with the music, Josh heard Jean gasp. He'd remember this moment for the rest of his life. Millions of people enjoyed music through SymphoCync, but none of them mattered more than the small, ecstatic person currently bouncing beside him.

He hadn't even realized he'd put his arm around Jonah until he felt Jean's arm rest atop his. *Complete* really was the only way to describe it. People called him successful all the time, and he was, but none of that ever felt like this.

When the song drew to a close, Jonah put the Jonah-phone in his lap, looked up at Josh with wide, excited eyes and banged the fingers of one hand resolutely in the palm of the other. Josh knew that sign. "Again, huh?"

Jonah repeated the sign—and the song—four more

times until Jean gave a laughing moan and said, "I think we're gonna need a bigger repertoire."

Josh joined her laughter. "You can turn off the audio."

"No," she said, her eyes glowing just the way Josh had hoped they would at this moment. "More songs sounds better."

He almost hated to ask, "Does he have favorites?"

"He couldn't," she replied softly. Josh felt his heart break wide open when she added, "until now." Her eyes glistened as she whispered, "I don't know how to thank you."

I do, he thought, but dared not say. This had to be her call.

He watched her gaze bounce between himself and Jonah for a moment before Jean said, "I think it's time."

Josh's stomach flipped. "Right now?"

"I think today's big enough already. I'm booked all morning getting ready for Violet's arrival. But tomorrow afternoon is the last chance I'll have any free time before the wedding. Let's take an hour and go fishing. We can release a 'Big Fish' for a better one."

He'd been a father for five years. He'd known he'd been one for only two weeks. And now tomorrow, he'd become a father to his son in the way that mattered most of all.

Chapter Fifteen

Jean found she understood now about how Josh had
been unable to concentrate at work. She'd made it
through the rest of Wednesday and all of this morning's frantic preparations, but her mind was elsewhere.
It was fixed on this hour, on this time as they stood
in the creek and fished. At the spot where Josh would
forever change in Jonah's eyes. It was another perfect
day, warm and sunny with a perfect breeze and fluffy
clouds. She took the ideal weather as God's blessing
on the huge shift about to happen.

Josh waded out of the water holding up his "prize
fish." They were in shallow enough water that simply
boots would have sufficed, but Josh once again appeared in his complete fisherman's ensemble, the can-
vas bucket hat cocked comically to one side. The only
nod to the man he was elsewhere was a brightly colored
SymphoCync T-shirt under the straps of his hip waders.

"Look at how big he is!" he boasted with ridiculous
pride. A mediocre-sized trout, it would have been a perfectly ordinary catch for any of the valley's residents,

but Josh's delight was amusing. He was having fun this afternoon, but she could tell he was on pins and needles until she did what they'd both come here to do.

On the bank beside her, Jonah alternated between applauding enthusiastically and signing "hooray!" while jumping up and down. She loved that his excitement for Josh was as large as his excitement over his own first fish had been. Jonah's heart was huge—he loved everyone instantly and without hesitation. The connection he'd made with Josh, however, exceeded even that gregarious nature. Even before the bond that the Jonahphone had brought, they knew each other in a way only blood could explain.

"So big! No keep?" Josh signed to Jonah with a face of exaggerated disappointment.

Jonah's enormous laugh and his "never" sign made Josh clutch at his heart and retaliate with repeated "big fish" signs. Clearly, Josh believed any man whose name sign was "Big Fish" could catch no "small fish."

Big Fish. It was maybe the last time he'd use that name. *Heavenly Father, watch over this moment*, Jean prayed as she watched Jonah and Josh release the flapping fish back into the water. *It's so important for all of us*.

She caught Josh's eye for a moment and nodded before she signed and voiced the words, "Jonah, honey, come sit down for a bit. I have something important to tell you."

Josh set down his rod, taking a nervous breath. It warmed her heart and bolstered her confidence that he wanted this so much. He would find a way to be more than a temporary or fringe fixture in Jonah's life, wouldn't he?

Jonah plopped down on the blanket she'd spread out, wearing a reluctant "aw, Mom" expression over the fact that she'd halted the antics with his new friend. That wouldn't last long. Josh settled carefully down opposite them.

She'd rehearsed this speech dozens of times, but all her carefully chosen words seemed to fly out of reach. How did you say something so large to someone so small?

She had planned to keep her eyes on Jonah, voicing her signs so that Josh could be part of the conversation, but Josh tapped her on the elbow. "I know the sign. I've practiced how to tell him. Lead up to it however you want, but please, Jean, let me. Let me tell him who I am." His voice cracked on the final words.

How could she deny him this moment? After all he had already done for Jonah? She nodded, then returned her gaze to Jonah. Despite her earlier peace, her heart hammered against her ribs now that the moment had arrived. She was grateful Jonah couldn't hear the shaking in her voice as she began. "Big Fish has become a good friend, yes?"

Jonah's oversize "yes!" sign made her pounding heart glow.

"You like him very much, and he likes you very much."

Jonah looked over at Josh, who smiled and signed, "Yes."

"Well," Jean continued, "Big Fish is an important

person in your life. More important than you know. He's always been a person in your life, actually."

Jonah's eyebrows scrunched up as he made the sign for "how?"

"Big Fish and I were friends…very good friends… long before you came along. He's been a special part of your life since before you were born, only you didn't know it. He didn't know it, either, for a bunch of grown-up reasons you don't need to worry about. Because you're both here, now, together, and all of us will be part of each other's lives from now on." She said that last bit while looking straight at Josh, casting it as the promise she'd demanded it be before she'd ever tell Jonah what she was about to tell him.

"You see, Big Fish has a different name, a special name, one that's important to you. And it's time that he got to tell you what that is."

Jonah followed Jean's gaze to Josh, his small eyes wide with curiosity. "What?" he signed.

Slowly, with a heartwarming seriousness, Josh spread his fingers wide and touched his thumb to his forehead. "I'm father." After a second, he expanded, adding the signs for "I'm your dad. You're my son."

Jean's throat tightened at the emotion in Josh's tone as he voiced the life-changing words. An excruciating pause hung in the air as Jean watched her son absorb what he'd heard. His small eyebrows furrowed together, and then his gaze bounced back and forth between her and Josh a few times. Both she and Josh nodded in acknowledgment of his silent query. She wanted to grab hold of every detail—from the green of the leaves to the way the sunlight slanted into the clearing to the sound of the creek behind them and Josh's nervous, shallow breaths across from her.

"You father?" Jonah signed to Josh. "My father?" Jean thought the sight of her son's hand on his chest, small fingers splayed against his heart in the sign for "my," might stay pressed against her own heart forever. She took a breath to translate, then fell silent, realizing Josh needed no translation.

There were days where the silence of the valley felt holy to her. The silence of this moment felt twice that— celestial, eternal, as if all of Heaven had peeked through the clouds to watch.

"Me." Josh's one-word reply was a broken, breathy sigh, followed by "Your father," signed with determined fingers. For some people, it took a long time before they could effectively convey emotion in sign. Josh had already mastered it.

"Really?" Jonah signed, mouth open and eyes wide.

"A little help here?" Josh asked nervously, nodding at the unfamiliar sign.

"He's asking 'really?'" she explained as a tear slid down her cheek. She wanted to both laugh and cry at the same time. The moment felt so big, it ought to hold twelve emotions, not just those two feelings.

"Yeah," Josh said as he repeated the sign back to Jonah with a heartbreakingly encouraging expression. "Really."

"Big Fish really is your father," Jean signed, failing to keep her own voice from catching with the tears that filled her eyes at the important words. "And he'll always be your father, from now on. You have a daddy now, Jonah. Are you happy about that?"

There was a hushed moment, the tiniest of pauses as she and Josh watched Jonah continue to absorb the enormous fact. She had never, until this moment, let herself consider that Jonah might not accept the news. Might resent it, even. He was so young, and he'd already been through so much in losing his grandfather—the only father figure he'd ever known, and barely known at that. Despite his bubbly personality, expressing his feelings had always been hard for Jonah. After all, he was so young, and emotions didn't always follow logic. She needed to make space for him to be upset instead of happy if that's what he needed, but she had no idea how. Was she helping her son? Or hurting him? *Oh, Lord, tell me—have I done the right thing?*

"Jonah…" Josh moaned the word, his agonized tone telling Jean that he felt all the same worries that gripped her heart. Josh had been so dismissed or pressured by his own father that it would rock him to the core to be rejected by his son. It struck her, at this moment that seemed to stretch on forever, that Josh would be a great father because it would crush him to repeat the faults of his own father.

It started as a small bubbling, a sparkle in Jonah's eyes that began slowly to ripple out through the rest of him. Jonah put his hands to his cheeks—his favorite show of amazement—with wide eyes and an open mouth. It was like watching a tiny fountain of joy surge and overflow its banks.

"Wow!" Jonah barely formed the sign as he flung himself at Josh, hugging and laughing and erupting in wildly happy sounds. The two fell backward, Josh's elated laughter holding the sounds of relief and more than a hint of tears.

"That's the sign for 'wow,'" she said over the noise, feeling her own fountain of tears surge and overflow.

"Wow," Josh repeated from somewhere inside the tumble of Jonah's arms and legs. "Wow." The world had tilted; something had forever changed. *We just became a family.* So what if it didn't look like the one she'd had or ones others had? Despite a host of complications and uncertainties, Jean felt less alone. The pang of abandonment she'd felt since Dad's passing eased up just a bit. Jonah had another champion in his corner—and a powerful one at that.

She let them tumble about in their father-son glee, reveling in the moment. *Thank you, Father. Thank you for this.* It felt as if her very bones offered up the gratitude. She felt her own wet lashes against her cheeks as her eyes closed, new tears sliding down her face.

Suddenly, the warmth of Josh's hand wrapped around hers, squeezing it tight. She opened her eyes to look at him and found she couldn't actually tell if Josh was laughing or crying. Did it really matter which? Still on his back, Jonah clinging atop him, Josh kept his hand tightly around Jean's while his other arm pressed his son to his chest. Jonah was still giggling, his small forehead pressed against Josh's so that their brown hair tumbled together. They looked so much like each other. They *were* so much like each other.

A sob of something too big for happiness or relief burst out of her, and she wiped her cheeks with one hand because Josh still had not let go of the other. Josh reacted to the sound, twisting his head to look at her with eyes that reflected everything she was feeling. Jonah picked up on the reaction, scrambling upright once he caught sight of his mother.

"Why cry?" he signed, scooting over to look at her quizzically.

"Happy," she signed. It seemed perfect that the sign was made with upward strokes from the heart. Her heart did feel as if it had fluttered upward, had lifted outward somehow. "I'm happy," she said for Josh's benefit as she repeated the sign.

"Happy, too," Jonah signed. He turned to Josh. "You?"

"Happy," Josh said.

"Daddy," Jonah signed, his hand touching his forehead where the sign was made.

"Yeah," Josh said and signed. "Daddy." Then, as if losing his nerve, he looked at Jean and said, "Tell him he can still call me Big Fish if that feels more comfortable to him. I don't want to force this."

She didn't realize she had been waiting for a signal that Josh would put Jonah's needs before his own. But it was there, in that single statement and the affection filling Josh's eyes.

"You get to choose," she signed to Jonah, voicing so that Josh could hear. "You can call him Big Fish or Daddy, whichever you want. This is new, and you don't have to decide now."

The "aw, Mom" look returned. "Daddy," Jonah repeated with a tiny little "no-brainer" face that made Jean laugh.

Jonah then made a sign that made Jean's heart still

in wonder. She lost her voice for a moment, amazed at the ease with which Jonah embraced his new world.

"What's that?" Josh asked, watching Jonah's fingers.

Jean smiled into Josh's eyes. "That's the sign for 'family.'"

She watched as Josh duplicated the sign, bringing his fingers around to join each other in a sort of circle. Then he and Jonah did it together.

When she joined in, so that all three of them made the sign simultaneously, she understood why circles were complete, even when they weren't perfect.

Chapter Sixteen

The wedding was here.

Or, more precisely, the bride was about to arrive.

Josh had helped Jean and everyone in the valley as much as he could, grateful for something else to think about other than the looming issue of Hal Braddon's offer. Matt checked in—impatiently—every day, and so far Braddon hadn't retracted his offer and even showed a tiny glimpse of impatience when Matt informed the man Josh was busy giving his stepsister away at her wedding.

Now, as he picked Violet and her maid of honor, Lucy, up from the airport, Josh felt surprisingly settled despite the nuptial whirlwind that was about to start.

"Lyle and all his family will be in later this afternoon. They rented a van to hold everyone. I can't wait to see the look on his mother's face when she sees where we are having the ceremony," Violet gushed, all eager and bubbly. "You, too, Lucy. It's gorgeous, isn't it Josh?"

"Really beautiful," Josh agreed, although he wasn't

even sure the two women heard him as they chatted happily over plans and details.

"Oh, and wait until you meet Mayor Jean. She's the mayor of the town and she runs the weddings—can you imagine? She and Josh go all the way back to college, and we didn't even know it until we visited earlier this month."

Josh marveled at Violet's ability to simplify what felt like a mountain of complicated history. "All the way back to college"? The way Violet said it made him feel rather ancient, despite that he wasn't even yet thirty. Still, that gave him a reminder of what this wedding meant to Jean, as well as to his stepsister. Jean was going to give Violet a spectacular wedding, he was sure of it. It was fun to be cheering for everyone involved, right down to the florist, the baker and the church janitor, "Boss," setting up the chairs.

No one ever called Boss by his real name, whatever it was, but he'd met the man getting breakfast one morning at Wanda's and they'd taken an immediate liking to each other. Boss had invited him to come back to church on more than just Potluck Sundays. Jean had invited him to church. Pastor Mitchell had invited him to church. With that level of evangelism he ought to feel surrounded, but instead it just felt like a great big circle of welcome.

"Did you eat on the plane?" Josh asked as he turned off the highway to the road that led into the valley. Something happened to his pulse every time he made that turn. A surprising combination of quickening and slowing—a peaceful eagerness, if that made any sense. It came over him every time he entered the valley, as though he physically registered the absence of the place and his return to it. "We could swing by Wanda's if you want, or I'm sure Hailey could send something up to your room."

"Listen to him," Violet remarked, "chatting about everyone like a local. He's become hung up on the place, Lucy, I tell you."

"Really?"

"Well, actually, he's a bit hung up on the mayor. They were a thing back in college."

Josh gave Violet a look that said "no more details" through the rearview mirror. Lucy and Violet had climbed in the back together so they could begin going over Violet's enormous bridal notebook on the drive. Honestly, he'd launched entire versions of software with less documentation.

"Really?" Lucy's voice held more curiosity than Josh would have liked.

"Don't press me for details—he's not sharing." That wasn't exactly true, but it served as a good out for Violet. He gave her a grateful look and continued driving. "Let's just go straight to the inn, Josh. I want to get unpacked before I take Lyle and his family out to the falls."

Josh pulled up to Hailey's Inn Love to see Jean standing at the entrance with a small bouquet of flowers. She was beaming. This was her big day, too, in many ways. Violet's wedding was a victory for everyone in Matrimony Falls, and that gave him reason to smile with every check he wrote. Money was fun. He was good at making it. Lots of people he knew were good at hoarding it, but Josh loved *using* it. Watching the things it made happen, the experiences it brought him, the ways it changed people's lives. This wedding was all that and Violet's happiness wrapped up in one event. The extraordinary circumstances that had led him to this weekend in this valley? Well, that was all just icing on the wedding cake.

Or providence, depending on whom you talked to. Josh was becoming more and more comfortable with his new possible position on Team Providence. The smile on his face as he ceremoniously opened the car door for Violet seemed to spread all the way to his fingertips. *Happy.* People always used that word, but never with the meaning as deep as he felt right now. *This is a happy time in a happy place. Does anyone here get how rare that is?*

"Hello, Violet!" Jean enveloped Violet in a huge hug, with Vi hugging her right back. "I'm so excited you're here!"

Lucy looked at him, surprised. He just shrugged, gave her a "yep, that's the way it is around here" look, and popped open the trunk to fetch the bags. Silicon Valley CEO turned chauffeur—would anyone back at SymphoCync believe it?

Introductions took a few seconds, and then Hailey appeared on the steps to sweep Violet and Lucy up to their rooms. Josh was grateful for the brief moments alone with Jean—his last chance for a while, he suspected.

"You did it," he said, daring to grab her hand. "Matrimony Valley's first bride is here for her wedding."

"I barely slept last night," Jean said, squeezing his hand. "And when I did sleep, I dreamed of all the things that could go wrong. I'm pretty sure an enormous mud-slide could not take over the falls and wash away the bride in a mountain of black dirt, but it made for a very unsettling nightmare."

"I'm sure." He laughed. "You'll be great. Everyone will be great. As chief bill payer, I think I'm entitled to give a little reassurance in that department."

Her eyes took on a soft glow. "You. Here. I mean, would you ever have believed it?"

"I'm changing the way I think about a lot of things, Jean." Why couldn't he be within ten feet of her anymore without having to tamp down the urge to kiss her? Now that he'd stepped into his role as Jonah's father, he was starting to want much more. Would the wedding about to surround them make that better, or worse?

The bliss of Violet's arrival lasted exactly three hours.

Kelly burst into Jean's office and pulled the door shut quickly behind her, her face filled with a wide-eyed panic. Something major was wrong.

This is the event business, she reminded herself. Things go wrong. But in the wedding business, things had to be put right for a happy bride. And not just right, but perfect. What bride ever wanted to look back on her special day and think, "We came pretty close"?

"Violet just called me in tears," Kelly began. "She wants all the flowers changed. On twenty-four hours' notice. On a holiday weekend."

Jean stood up and came around the desk. "What? Wasn't she dead set on purple irises?"

"She was. I bent over backward to find her purple

irises. And now, with no time left, she wants all tulips. Absolutely no irises, and nothing in purple. Forget the fact that it's going to cost a fortune. I'm not even sure it's possible."

Perhaps it was a blessing that Josh was already here. As the man writing the check, maybe he could be persuaded to talk Violet down off this particular floral ledge. Only Violet hadn't really struck her as the kind to change her mind on the fly. There had to be a reason—and it felt like an emotional one, if she had to guess. "Any idea why?"

Kelly collapsed into the guest chair. "Oh, there's a reason. I'm sure of it. This was some sort of emotional crisis thing—bigger than wedding jitters. But I don't have the faintest idea what it is, and she's not talking."

All the more reason to speak to Josh. "How can I help?"

Kelly nodded to the desk outside Jean's office. "Can I borrow Cathy for the afternoon? I'll need her to cover the register—it's going to take me all afternoon on the phone and the internet to track down what Violet wants."

"Of course." Young Cathy Bolton divided her time between serving as the town secretary and counter help at Kelly's shop. Usually, demand was never so pressing that the dual roles collided. Maybe that wouldn't be the case for much longer. Jean added it to the ever-growing mental list of adjustments to be made as Matrim's Valley grew into Matrimony Valley.

"And then there's the cost," Kelly went on. "This is going to triple her bill. Maybe more. I've got to tell her that, but I don't think she'll hear it. Not right now. What do we do?"

"Why don't I put in a phone call to Josh. He may be able to shed some light on the drama—or at least take it down a notch."

"Good idea." Kelly's arched eyebrow asked a dozen questions about Josh that Jean didn't have time to answer at the moment.

Jean picked up her cell phone, intending to text Josh and ask him to walk over from the inn. "Anything else?"

"Not unless you can produce tulips out of thin air by tomorrow." Kelly rolled her eyes and put her hand to her forehead. "Not exactly Bridezilla, but…"

"I have a feeling there's something at work here," Jean said. "Give me an hour to see if I can get to the bottom of it before you kill yourself hunting down last-minute replacements." She typed My office ASAP? Re: V and hit Send.

"I'll let you know what I discover. I'll send Cathy over as soon as she finishes a set of school board documents."

"Great."

Kelly was barely out the door when Jean's phone let out a ding and showed Josh's reply: On my way. Everything OK?

She typed Not sure. She'd have brushed her hair and freshened her lipstick for anyone, she told herself as she waited for Josh's appearance.

He pushed through her door just a few minutes later, a concerned look on his face. "What'd Vi do?"

"She sent Kelly into a fit by completely changing

her floral order. Absolutely no purple irises, after insisting on them. Out of the blue. Do you have any idea what's behind this? Because Kelly will try and make it happen, but she's worried the bill will shock you."

Josh sank into the chair much the same way Kelly had. "I did this."

Jean couldn't quite work out how that could have happened. "You want to tell me how?"

Josh ran both hands through his hair. "You know Violet knows about Jonah."

What did that have to do with a drastic last-minute floral crisis? "Yes. I thought you told me she was really supportive about it."

"She was. She is," Josh replied. "She's been all gushy and happy about it, and how I'll make a great dad. But you know Vi. She goes overboard."

Jean sat in the chair opposite him. "I still don't see what this has to do with flowers."

Josh pinched the bridge of his nose. "She was going on again before Lyle and his family got here. Talking about fatherhood got her talking about my dad. Vi loved my dad. She didn't have all the baggage I had with him, you know? They were close. I think maybe his death hit her harder than it hit me, even though he was her stepfather." When he seemed to sense Jean still didn't make the connection, he offered, "Purple irises were Dad's favorite. That's why she wanted them. She said they would make her feel like he was there."

This was heading to a dangerous place. "Oh," she said, noting the regret in Josh's eyes.

"She was going on and on about missing Dad, and that's not my favorite subject these days, as you can imagine. So I don't know what came over me. She was putting him on such a pedestal, and it was getting to me. I might have...told her what he did to you."

There had been a time when only two people on earth knew what Bartholomew Tyler had done. There had been a time, after his death, when she carried that knowledge alone. Now it felt like an ever-widening ripple, sending shock waves out across the water in all directions.

It all comes home to roost. Over and over.

"Oh, no." How strangely all their lives intersected—no, tangled—now. She was beginning to see how God could transform this situation into a kind of good, but that didn't entirely outrun the widening circle of pain. Funny how she'd always seen the "Matrimony Valley" concept as bringing happiness into the valley. It would, she hoped, but today it was hard to see how they got there from here.

"She's upset. I upset her. I don't think she ever thought of Dad as someone capable of that. It's always bothered me, how she saw him. I resented it, I suppose, how he never seemed to show that side of himself to her. As though she were exempt from the demands I was under." He slumped back in the chair. "On some level, I think I knew what it would do to her to learn what he'd done. And I told her anyway. Today of all days." He looked over at Jean. "Why did I do that? What was the point of her knowing? She didn't need to know—I had no right to taint her memory of him. Couldn't I have just let her have her happiness?"

Jean sighed. "Pain never feels fair. No one wants more than their share. I could have let Bartholomew's sins die with him, but I didn't. I know it explained my silence in some ways, but I also admit there was some selfish revenge in watching you hurt the way I had."

Josh's eyes darkened. "It's not the same. You had every right to tell me. It's important that I know. It shocked me that he'd go to that length, do that to you and to Jonah, but I can't say it surprised me. I knew what kind of man my father was. You didn't taint my view of him."

"And now you've tainted Violet's view of her father."

"Tainted? I think Kelly's trashed flower order tells us I've done a bit more than that. It's like she can't even stomach the idea of his memory at her wedding now. I didn't have any right to do that, even if it is the truth."

Jean leaned on the chair arm. "We're all just trying to make sense of this, Josh. We all feel like we've been blindsided. It's hard to take the route of grace when we're still reeling ourselves."

"But this is Vi and her wedding. This is Matrimony Valley's first bride. This isn't supposed to be about me, and I made it about me." He shook his head. "How do I fix this?"

"Let's start with you talking to Violet. Get Lyle to talk to her. This is about much more than which flowers are at the ceremony. Help her work through her emotions."

Josh laughed. "Sure. Right after I figure out mine." He held Jean's gaze again, still with that unmoored look that caught her up short. "What do we do here, Jean? I've been a first-class jerk, and I don't know how to fix it."

Jean straightened, willing herself into uncharted waters. "I know what my dad would say if he were here."

"What's that?"

"Sometimes God takes us to a place where we have no answers to remind us that He does."

"That sounds like something your dad would say." He raised a dark eyebrow. "Do you believe that?"

She sighed. "I don't believe in coincidences." She waved her hand in the air between them. "All this is too much to be chance, don't you think?"

"Are you asking me if I think God's behind my appearance in Matrimony Valley?"

She paused for a moment, wanting to get the words right. "I'm asking you if it makes any sense any other way. Surely even you can see the divine design in this, how it's far too particular to be random."

It pleased her that he didn't brush off the notion. She could see him reach out, pushing his brilliant intellect to wrap around such an idea. "It's getting a little hard to ignore, I'll grant you that."

"Go talk to Violet. Help her see that what your father may have planned for bad still worked out for good. That what Bartholomew did to you doesn't change who he was for her. Maybe that will help calm her down."

"And if it doesn't?"

She gave him a thin smile. "Then get your checkbook ready, because if she still wants to change her flowers, it's going to cost you plenty."

Chapter Seventeen

Matrimony Valley's first-ever bride could not have looked more beautiful. Or more nervous. Jean helped the maid of honor, Lucy, get Violet's veil just right as she stood on the flagstone path just out of view of the gathered guests.

The past twelve hours had been a flurry of last-minute crises large and small—four vegetarian guests who'd "forgotten" to note their preferences on their RSVP cards, one bridesmaid's dress that sustained a rip, two missed flights resulting in guests who wouldn't make the ceremony but would arrive in time for the reception—and a monumental compromise from irises to tulips to lilies. Everything was as perfect as it was going to be to join the lives of Captain Lyle Davis and Violet Ann Thomas in front of the Matrimony Falls.

Josh seemed a bastion of calm Jean wasn't entirely sure he felt. Then again, scrambling to make deadlines was part of what he did. He'd told her at last night's rehearsal dinner that more than once he'd been onstage hyping up a product's release, fully aware the engineers were backstage making a mad dash to ensure it all worked. None of that quite covered the guilt she knew he held for blurting out a truth that should have stayed hidden for another day, if not forever.

The regret softened him, turned him in tender attention to his stepsister. Jean watched him squeeze Violet's hand with a surprisingly gentle affection in his eyes. "It's easy from here. Even if twenty-five things go wrong, at the end of this hour you'll be Mrs. Lyle Davis. That's what you came here to do. Everything else is just fringe."

Violet adjusted the string of pearls around her neck—a gift from Josh—for the fifth time. "Easy for you to say," she quipped to her stepbrother. "I feel a bit sick. What if I trip?"

"I'll be here to catch you," Josh said, his voice smooth and reassuring.

"What if Lyle hates the dress?"

Josh grinned. "Speaking on behalf of every male in a five-hundred-mile radius, Lyle will not hate the dress. You look incredible. Your biggest problem might be getting him to speak or keep upright, you look so beautiful. Stop worrying. Let me walk you down this aisle to those beautiful falls where Lyle is waiting."

With that, Jean stepped out to where the harpist could see her signal to begin the music. At the appointed cue, Jean sent the first bridesmaid around the corner and down the flagstone path toward the gazebo. Her heart swelled a bit at the oohs and aahs of the guests. The tilt of the morning sun perfectly hit the daisy-yellow bridesmaids' gowns so that they fairly glowed. She knew the hint of sparkle in Violet's gown would catch the sun with even more splendor. Josh was right; Lyle was in for a stunning first view of his bride.

One by one, each bridesmaid made her way down the aisle to stand opposite the row of dashing navy seamen in their snappy dress blues. At the bottom of the aisle, Lyle stood in dress whites with the same anxious-yet-thrilled smile that currently beamed under Violet's veil.

While never meaning to, Josh stood out himself as the only civilian member of the bridal party in a white dinner jacket. Josh didn't often wear suits, but when he did, the man looked astounding. Lyle's astonishment had nothing on the breath that left her when she first saw Josh in his formal attire, or the glow that lit in her chest when he smiled just for her.

"Let's go get you married," he said in a gentle voice to Violet. "Just start walking and hang on to me." With that, he pulled her gently in motion, and the pair turned the corner to begin their walk down the aisle.

Jean watched them pass, listening with grateful bliss at the reaction of the guests as the sun did indeed catch Violet's dress and set it sparkling. She knew that somewhere behind her, a host of valley residents were spreading tablecloths, setting tables and plating hors d'oeuvres. Yet another last-minute brigade was likely shuttling lily centerpieces to Hailey's Inn as fast as Kelly could assemble them. Poor Kelly probably had gotten less sleep last night than she had, and that was saying something. Still, despite the frantic "backstage" scramble, Jean allowed herself a quiet confidence that most of the guests had no idea anything had gone wrong. And that was how it should be.

She watched Josh reach the bottom of the aisle with Violet. His broad smile touched her heart as he lifted Violet's veil and kissed her cheek. Thankful Violet had Josh to give her away, Jean wondered for a painful moment who would give her away if she ever made the walk down this aisle as a Matrimony Valley bride. Would it be so long in coming that Jonah would be old enough to do the honors?

Josh placed Violet's hand into that of her groom and took his seat in the first row. *I wish I could see his face,* she thought, *watch him as he watches the ceremony.* Would he project himself—or the two of them—into the ceremony the same way she did? Did he wonder what their wedding would have been like, the same way she had since that conversation four nights ago on the mountain?

Had he come to feel for her as strongly as she'd come to feel for him? It didn't matter whether it was wise or foolish; today heightened the feelings she had for him. Maybe it was best she couldn't lose herself in the dazzle of his gaze right now—the mayor and chief wedding planner of Matrimony Valley had too much to do.

That didn't stop her heart from skipping a beat as Pastor Mitchell began, "Dearly beloved, we are gathered here today…"

"I now pronounce you man and wife. Friends, may I present to you Captain and Mrs. Lyle Davis."

Josh broke into thunderous applause along with the other wedding guests. Drawn silver swords flashed in the sunlight to create a ceremonial bridge under which Lyle and Violet took their first steps up the aisle as husband and wife. The joy in the place blazed full and energizing. Josh felt the stress of his life slough off his shoulders, at least for the next few hours. Today was a day to celebrate how love and happiness still showed up in the world.

He looked around for Jean as the guests filed out of the clearing, aware she was probably off coordinating some detail of the transition from ceremony to reception. Being one of the last guests to leave the space, he turned to gaze again at the cascade of water that served as Violet's backdrop. Truly, no church he could think of—even the charming little sanctuary in the valley's church—could match the splendor of the falls. Who could fault Jean for wanting to get married here? For helping other people get married here?

I'd want to get married here.

I'd want to marry Jean here.

He did. He'd been fighting the growing sense of wanting to be part of Jean's life for days now. It wasn't the desire to make it happen that was lacking; it was just the logistics of making it work. The things it might cost him. Things that, up until he'd stepped out of that car with Violet on Aisle Avenue, seemed vastly important. It wasn't that they weren't important anymore— the employees of SymphoCync, the career he'd built, the things he'd made possible—it was that he'd discovered some things that were more important. Some people who were more important.

How? he asked the falls—or, more precisely, their Creator. *How do I do this impossible thing?*

The answer struck him as he turned to walk up the petal-strewn aisle and make his way to the reception: *the same way you've done all the other impossible things in your life.*

That's not entirely true, some new and deep part of him he suspected Jean would call his soul argued. *You can't do this. But the God who makes all things possible can, if you're willing to ask.*

Okay, God, he replied to himself, realizing with a start that what he was doing could be qualified as praying. *I'm asking.*

Chapter Eighteen

Less than an hour later, Josh watched his stepsister dance with her new husband. As she twirled with Lyle in the center of the dining room of Hailey's Inn Love, her face still glowed with the wonder of the ceremony.

It was more than just wedding day bliss. He'd thought about it since handing her off to her new husband at the end of the aisle: she'd become complete. Lyle completed Vi, and she did the same for her captain. It was what made words like *soul mate* make sense. As Lyle grinned at his wife, Josh found himself grinning with happiness for his stepsister. Some people really were destined for each other.

The thought sent his gaze around the room until he found Jean, standing slightly apart from the crowd. He'd never tell the bride, but Jean was by far the most beautiful woman in the building. Not in the eye-catching way she was in college—although she still was gorgeous in his estimation—but in a deeper, lasting kind of beauty. The grace and strength he'd seen from her this month had an allure beyond the color of her eyes or the dazzle of her smile. *I need her. I'll never not need her. I'll never be right without her.* No pressure, no demand or ultimatum, but the ease of certainty. A truth more powerful than anything Hal Braddon could ever offer.

Jonah, standing next to Jean in an adorable blue striped seersucker jacket and a jaunty bow tie, wiggled his fingers in a wave. *Him, too*, his heart pronounced. Somehow, without his even realizing it, Jean and Jonah had taken the spot at the center of his life he'd always allowed SymphoCync to occupy. When did that happen? He couldn't go back to how it was a year ago even if he wanted to. And he didn't want to.

He walked over to where they were standing. Jonah's enthusiastically signed "Hi, Dad" shot a glow of joy through him that could have challenged Violet's bliss to a contest.

"Hi, J," he signed. "Let's dance with Mom."

Jonah scrunched up his face with the expected reaction of his age to dancing with grown-ups. "It'll be fun," Josh insisted, adding a grin as he heard Jean chuckle from behind him.

Jonah replied by sticking out his tongue.

"Maybe he'd rather go help me find some cookies," Bill Williams said, appearing from out of nowhere and making the sign for "cookies" while he cast a knowing glance between Josh and Jean. "Dancing's boring." He added something else Josh didn't recognize, but it clearly convinced Jonah.

"What did Bill say?" Josh asked as he led Jean to the dance floor. When Jean slid into his arms, it was as if all the years since they'd last danced evaporated like the mountain mist in sunshine.

"Nothing," she replied.

He chose to let it slide, reluctant to do anything that would mar the delicacy of the moment. He had Jean Matrim in his arms. The amazement of that wasn't likely to leave him for a long time—if ever. "You know," he said with a more intimate tone than he would have dared even yesterday, "I still can't quite get over the fact that I'm here."

Her eyes sparkled. "At your sister's wedding?"

"Well, that, too." Jean's gaze left his eyes for a moment, settling on the blissful newlyweds he knew were dancing behind them. Sure, this day belonged to Violet and Lyle, but today was a milestone for Jean, as well. "Congratulations, Mayor Matrim. You pulled it off. You made Matrimony Valley."

Her face flushed at the compliment—he'd always loved that about her. Back in the day, he used to tell her over and over how beautiful she was just to watch it light the glow in her cheeks. "God made Matrimony Valley, not me."

"Oh, I disagree. God made Matrim's Valley, but you made Matrimony Valley. I ought to have my PR guys write you up a press release. 'Jean Matrim single-handedly saves hometown.' The world loves a good turnaround story."

He felt her soften in his hands just the smallest bit more against him, and it sent a zing down his spine. "Oh, I think God made Matrimony Valley, too," she said, her tone a little more breathless. "I pleaded with Him for a solution, and the idea came to me not long after." Hadn't he just done the same thing not an hour ago? He wanted her to rest her head against his shoulder the way he remembered her doing. Her head on his shoulder was the most exquisite feeling in the world. Instead, she turned her face to look right at him. "Can you believe in something like that?"

"I never thought I would," he replied, not stopping himself from pulling her even closer. This new strength of hers called to him in irresistible ways. The contentment that radiated from her, from Lyle and Vi, seemed to seep right out of the forest and into new corners of him.

Contentment. He'd always considered it the opposite of ambition, but that wasn't it at all.

"But now?"

"I'm gonna say something stupid," he said, unable and unwilling to stop the foolish grin he could feel spreading across his face.

"You're too brilliant to say anything stupid," she replied.

Oh, he could think of a few truly foolhardy things to say at this moment with her looking at him like that. "Well, unexpected, then." He pulled in a deep breath, suddenly aware of her heartbeat against his. "I feel like…like my soul…woke up here."

He waited for her to laugh at the sugary sentiment, but instead her smile just glowed all the more. "The valley does that. But only to the person who's ready for it."

He was ready for it. Who back in San Jose would believe that? "I see why you fight so hard to keep it going. Jonah deserves to have this." With a surge of bravado he added, "I'm glad our son has this." He wondered how much longer he'd be able to resist saying "I want this." Right now, it felt like he wouldn't last the hour.

Ah, but Jean was still the kind of woman who never let him get away with anything. "And what about you?"

Last an hour? He clearly wasn't going to last the next sixty seconds. His newly awakened soul told him to tell the truth. "What I think I want is at war with what's possible." That was it in one sentence, wasn't it?

Her eyes told him she understood the full breadth of what he said. "Joshua Tyler, you've been at war with what's possible as long as I've known you."

"I don't always win," he admitted. It struck him that he'd never voiced that to anyone before, not even Matt. It was his role to reframe every defeat with words that played better, words like *temporary setback* or *challenge we can meet*. One thing he wasn't winning—wasn't even sure he wanted to win anymore—was the battle to stay away from the valley, to resist the lure of the land around him and the woman in front of him. But that wouldn't be losing, would it? He'd be gaining so much. Jean. Jonah. They were more valuable than a dozen Hal Braddons, despite his deep pockets and endless influence. What was here felt eternal. As if the logistics of how he held on to it were mere details.

Jean seemed to catch on to his thoughts, for she raised an eyebrow and asked, "What?"

Josh let the hand on Jean's back wander up to play with a tendril of hair that had escaped her businesslike, mayoral and wedding planner updo, luxuriating in what came over her eyes when he did. Pulling her hair down out of its ponytail used to be his definition of bliss.

"I was just thinking how tiny San Jose feels right now. The valley feels huge, and everything back in California feels like a tiny detail."

* * *

She'd fallen back in love with him. Or the love had never really left, just "woken up," the way he said his soul had. He held her the way he used to, but then again altogether differently. Back then it was she who circled around his brilliance, riding the tail of his rising star. Now, it was an equal thing, born of respect. And born of what they were to Jonah.

"Come home, Josh." The words escaped her lips before she could recognize their recklessness. And it was reckless to invite him to the valley. To ask him to do the impossible. But she suspected that didn't stop either of their hearts from wanting it. She could always read him, and the yearning in his eyes was so much stronger now than the lost look he'd borne when he first stepped out of the car with Violet.

She watched her words hit him. His shoulders tightened under her arm as it rested on him, and his eyes widened—in what? Shock? Recognition? Agreement? His arms pulled her close.

"I don't know if I know how." His admission sounded as if it bared his soul. She'd never known Josh Tyler to admit he didn't know anything. He was a "never give in, never give up" force of ambition. It had been that power that first drew her to him, but Jean realized that with those words, he'd finally, fully stolen her heart.

"I didn't know how or if my plan would save the valley, either."

"So you're saying I should plead with the Almighty to help me pull this off?"

"I'm saying you should ask the God who loves you to bring you home to the son who loves you, too."

"I love him," Josh said with a fierce glow in his eyes. "I think I loved him from the first moment he handed me his truck. Is that possible?"

"Of course it is." Hadn't she loved Jonah from the first moment she became aware of his existence? And more the moment his sweet eyes first looked up into hers? Eyes that were so very much like Josh's eyes, which burned into hers right now?

Those eyes glinted with mischief. "How much of a scandal would it cause if I kissed you right here, right now in front of everybody?"

She giggled like a schoolgirl. "Let's find out."

"Yes, ma'am, Your Honor."

Chapter Nineteen

The morning after the reception, Josh felt drawn back to the falls. Despite Jean's insistence that God was everywhere, to Josh He seemed to reside here. The grandeur of the falls and the surrounding nature were a far more fitting "church" to Josh than all the breathtaking cathedrals he had seen on his travels—not that he was in the habit of visiting holy places. Still, after watching Violet and Lyle vow the rest of their lives to each other yesterday with such bliss on their faces, this did seem like a holy place.

The chairs were still set out; the colored ribbons still fluttered in the breeze down the aisle and around the gazebo. He laughed to himself as he sat down in one of the chairs—this sort of stuff would have been gone in an hour if left outside overnight in San Jose. He remembered looking down from his hotel window at one outdoor wedding in Los Angeles to note with sad amusement that the chairs had been strung through with airplane cable and a padlock.

Not here. In Matrimony Valley, no one owned a

car alarm, bicycles were never locked and he couldn't say if people even locked their front doors. More than once, he'd ducked into a business on Aisle Avenue to find the place unattended and a "Back in five minutes" note posted to the counter. The whole town felt decent and human and caring—and that, he realized, is what drew him back. Who'd have thought decent and human and caring would win out over fast, loud and exciting? Certainly not the Josh Tyler he'd been a month ago.

A loud sound caused him to turn around, and he saw Kelly Nelson, the florist, picking up one of the large tin urns that had been set at the top of the aisle. There was a little girl with her—her daughter, he realized, having met them at the florist shop while trying to calm Violet down about the whole last-minute flower crisis.

"Oh, sorry, I didn't see you there," Kelly said as she set the urn upright. "I can come back later."

"No," Josh said as he rose. "You're not disturbing me. I just wanted to see the place again." He walked toward her. Poor Kelly—she'd pulled off an amazing feat of logistics to make the flowers for this wedding happen. "You must be exhausted, but you did a great job on your first wedding. I know Vi didn't make it easy on you."

Kelly undid the string that tied a bunch of ribbon to one of the chairs. "All brides are complicated."

"I don't think all brides make huge last-minute flower switches on holiday weekends, though, do they?"

"Well, if you've got the money for it, most problems are solvable." She gave Josh a look as she handed the brightly colored loops to her daughter. "Sorry it cost you so much to give your sister what she wanted. I did the best I could on crazy short notice like that. I didn't gouge you, I promise."

"I never thought you did. I was actually impressed you pulled it off in so short a time." He undid the string from the bunch of ribbon on the chair nearest him, handing it to the little girl.

"Thanks," she said brightly. "I'm Lulu."

For a split second, Josh thought about all the times Jonah missed a simple exchange like this. His heart gave in to a moment's ache for all the ways Jonah was cut off from the world. And yet, Jonah was more connected here than Josh had ever felt in San Jose. "Hi, Lulu, I'm Josh."

"That's Mr. Josh to you, hon. He walked our bride down the aisle, remember?"

Lulu smiled at the memory. "She was beautiful."

"She was, wasn't she?" Violet had glowed with love and happiness. She deserved it, and he really was overjoyed for her. Despite his error, yesterday had still been the happy day it was supposed to be. But yesterday had also unlocked a craving for love and happiness for himself.

Kelly leaned down to her daughter. "Why don't you collect all the ribbons in a great big bouquet for me?"

"Sure!" Lulu skipped off down the aisle on her collecting mission.

"So," Kelly said, facing him with a matter-of-fact expression. "You and Jean."

He'd kissed her in front of everyone at the reception last night—it shouldn't surprise him that someone was going to say something to him about it. "We…um… go back."

"I know," Kelly said. "I know everything, actually. About Jonah, and all." She paused for a moment. "I realize it may be none of my business, but we all love Jean, and she's been through a lot. No one wants to see her or Jonah hurt."

He hoped anyone at SymphoCync would stick up for him so fiercely, but he found he couldn't be sure. "I don't want to hurt either of them. I just want to be part of their lives here."

"Part? No offense, but I happened to be there and that kiss didn't look like it had anything partial about it. I don't know how they do things where you're from, but here in the valley, if you kiss a girl like that in front of everybody, you'd better mean it."

"I did mean it," he said defensively, then realized he didn't quite know what that declaration meant. "I care a lot about her."

Kelly looked down the aisle to her daughter. "Lulu's father was killed in an aviation accident. She knows he's gone. Every day she knows it, and misses him. I'd give anything—*anything*—to change that, but I can't."

"What are you saying?"

"I'm saying you have a choice with Jonah. He's such an amazing kid. Jean's a rare woman. Neither of them deserves only part. Don't lead her on to something you can't really give. Jonah needs a dad beside him, and Jean's not the kind of person who can ever do things halfway. She's poured her heart and soul into this town, and I just want to keep that heart from being broken."

"Wow," Josh said, rocking back on his heels. "No sugarcoating in Matrimony Valley, is there?"

"We're straight shooters, and we take care of our own." She smiled. "And I like you. And Jonah adores you. And Jean, well, I think it's pretty clear how she feels about you. I know you've got a lot waiting for you back in California. I just want to make sure you realize how much is waiting for you here."

It seemed to just leap out of him, even though he barely knew the woman. "What if I end up hurting them? What if I do…what it might take to be with them and it…fails?"

He waited for Kelly to roll her eyes at his blurted words, but she smiled gently and thought a moment before replying. "I know it sounds cheesy, but I think the only real failure to be afraid of here is the one you'd make by not trying. You're already his dad. It's just a question of what kind of dad you decide to be." Her thumb strayed to her empty ring finger, reminding Josh she was a widow and that her late husband's choice—and chance—had been stolen from him.

Not being around to watch Jonah enter middle school, or go to prom, or go to college and fall madly in love—the thought chewed at him in ways he'd never expected. "Does it ever get less terrifying—being a parent, that is?"

She looked at her daughter with the same mix of pride, worry and affection that often sat on Jean's face. "Actually, I think it gets worse. I mean, teenagers. And yeah, I think it will be different—harder, maybe—with Jonah. But I've never met a kid more up to the challenge. Ever think he might get that from you?"

It was true, he'd seen much of his own dogged problem-solving in Josh, his knack for pulling people into his world that was one of the key ingredients in SymphoCync's success. Josh was challenged in unique ways, but he was also amazing in ways that were just as unique. Still… "I think he gets a lot of that from his mother."

She laughed softly. "That's just as scary, isn't it?" Looking down at the gazebo where Violet had said her vows not twenty-four hours earlier, she continued. "Jean says weddings are the ultimate act of faith and optimism. That's why she did it, you know. Matrimony Valley."

"How so?"

"We were dying. When the mill closed and the jobs disappeared, so many people lost hope. We needed faith and optimism. We needed to *become* faith and optimism. That's why we're Matrimony Valley, and not 'Golf Valley' or 'Antiques Valley.'"

Every time he thought Jean could not amaze him more… "She never told me that."

Lulu had started coming back up the aisle, nearly swallowed by a huge collection of ribbons. "You should have heard her presentation to the town council. She had an uphill battle all the way, but she just kept going until she convinced them. I like to think of Violet as living proof that she was right." She looked down at her daughter. "Look at you! You got them all."

Lulu stuck her chin up over the mountain of satin strips. "It was hard, but I did it."

Kelly looked up at Josh. "You can say that about lots of things in life, sweetie." She picked up the box.

"Pile all those pretty ribbons in here and you can hang them up all over your room if you like. Miss Violet—excuse me, Mrs. Davis—is done with them." Returning her gaze to Josh, she said, "It's the prettiest spot in the valley. Good for thinking. Take all the time you need, and just stop by the church when you're done so Boss knows to come pick up the chairs."

"Bye!" Lulu waved.

As he waved back, Josh remembered a wave goodbye was the same in spoken English or sign. And that way back when SymphoCync was just a bunch of diagrams on paper, people had called him an impossible optimist, too.

He'd been mostly certain up until that moment. But as he sat there in the leafy cathedral that was Matrimony Falls, Josh decided he wanted the faith and optimism that thrived here. He wanted the woman and boy who thrived here as well, and it was time to win his own uphill battle with Hal Braddon.

If You really are the God who brought me here, be the God who keeps me here.

There was something about this valley. About the people. Something that was such a polar opposite of San Jose, he couldn't even begin to explain it.

He knew he'd only experienced it.

You can only experience it.

Josh pulled his phone from his pocket and dialed.

"Is Violet married?" Matt's voice was sleepy. It was pretty early out there given the time difference.

"Went off without a hitch—well almost." He decided to save the story of Violet's last-minute floral fiasco for another day. "What's your schedule look like for Tuesday?"

"Why?" Matt sounded suspicious.

"Because I think Tuesday sounds like a really good day for a promotion."

Matt yawned. "The marketing campaign for the launch has been in place for weeks. We don't need any more promotion."

"Not SymphoCync. You."

He could hear Matt sit up straight from wherever he was. "Huh?"

"I think I've found a way to do the deal."

"There is a way to do the deal. We say yes to Braddon's offer." Matt paused for a long moment before asking, "Are you saying you don't want to sell?"

"I'm saying I have a counteroffer in mind."

"Now I'm really confused."

"How would the title co-CEO clear things up?" Josh surprised himself to realize he was smiling.

"You want to make me co-CEO with you? Seriously?"

"You deserve it, Matt. And I'm going to need you if this is going to work out the way I want it to. Are you up for it?"

Josh could imagine Matt's wide eyes as he ran his hands through his hair. He'd likely jumped up and began pacing the room, if Josh knew his friend. "Co-CEO. With you."

"But we'd still have to convince Braddon to go along with it, so that's why I'm asking about Tuesday."

"I can do Tuesday," Matt agreed, still sounding a bit shocked.

"Matt?"

"Yeah?"

"Is that a yes?"

"Absolutely. It's absolutely a yes. But what am I doing Tuesday?"

"Bring Braddon to the valley. I mean it—charter a plane, charm his assistant, pull strings, whatever. Just find some way to bring Hal Braddon to Matrimony Valley for a couple of days—for just twenty-four hours, even. I can do the rest."

"Are you crazy? He won't."

"Then figure out a way so he will. We'll do it together. I'll send him an email with the most persuasive invitation I've ever written. You just make sure he says yes." Josh started walking back to town. If he could talk Bill Williams into opening up for him after lunch on a Sunday, it was time for another extravagant purchase.

"You've lost your marbles." Matt laughed nervously. "You know that, don't you?"

"No, just the opposite. I think I've found them. Pack your bags and call me back when you've got Braddon."

Josh clicked off the line. Tonight he would sit down to write the most important email of his life.

Big Fish was about to cast a line for the biggest fish of all.

Chapter Twenty

Memorial Day spent barbecuing in Jean's backyard was one of the most satisfying afternoons in Josh's memory. Jonah taught him all kinds of new words, and they spent hours in Jean's hammock filling the Jonah-phone with silly songs and happy pop tunes. The whole day settled so calm and convicting in Josh's gut that by sunset he had no doubt what his path must be from here.

So despite the size of the stakes in play, Josh felt solid and steady on Tuesday as he watched a nervous Matt and a curious Hal Braddon descend the staircase out of a private jet. Each held the gear bags Bill Williams had helped Josh Express Mail, to be waiting on the plane when they boarded. The wary look on both men told Josh they had opened the bags in flight, per his instructions.

"What's with the recreational theatrics?" Matt asked when he reached Josh first. "I was done with field trips in the third grade."

"Humor me," Josh said with more confidence than he felt.

"I hope you know what you're doing," Matt said. "'Cause I sure don't."

Hal Braddon walked up to Josh, nodding in greeting since his hands were full with the large bag. "You've got a flair for the dramatic, I'll give you that."

Josh laughed. "Have you ever been to North Carolina, Hal?"

Braddon set down the bag. "I've been stuck in the Charlotte airport a time or two, back when I flew commercial."

Josh doubted Hal Braddon had seen a coach airline seat in a while. "I needed you to see this before we struck a deal." He knew "struck" implied a bit more equal footing than he had here, but this was no time to be timid.

"You needed to take me on a fishing trip before I bought your business? Or did you just want to be the first person to ever kidnap me to seal a deal?"

Josh gestured to the sedan idling behind him, popping the trunk. He relieved the men of their gear bags, then he doubled back to stow their suitcases as well before sliding behind the wheel.

"Lunch is on your seats, gentlemen," he said as his passengers settled themselves in the back seat. On each of the seats was an ordinary brown paper bag from Watson's Diner.

Hal laughed as he opened up the bag. "I haven't had a BLT since high school."

"No turkey bacon nonsense," Josh replied. "That's real bacon from a cast-iron pan, not a microwave."

"White bread," Matt marveled. "I'd forgotten the stuff existed."

"There'll be pie and coffee at the creek later." He caught Hal's eyes in the rearview mirror. "When's the last time you had pie and coffee, Hal?"

"Can't remember," Hal replied after a hefty bite of Wanda's creation. "But I suspect I'm about to be reminded."

A short while later, the sedan pulled up to the intersection at the top of Aisle Avenue, where Mayor Matrim stood ready to welcome her newest batch of VIPs. It was a poignant echo of how this whole thing began, and one that chimed with certainty in Josh's chest, not apprehension. "May I present Mayor Jean Matrim."

"Welcome to Matrimony Valley, gentlemen." Even though he knew she had to be as nervous as he was, Jean's greeting held only a smooth, warm confidence.

Matt stepped back while Braddon shook Jean's hand. "The lady mayor of Matrimony Valley. This is getting interesting. And who are you, young fella?"

Hal bent down and extended a hand to Jonah. Josh stepped up, willing confidence into his voice—and fingers—as well. "Hal," Josh said and signed. "This is my son, Jonah." The words felt heavy with importance.

Hal looked surprised. "Your son? I didn't know."

Neither did I, Josh thought as he caught Jean's proud expression.

"How do I say hello?" Hal asked, a rare bit of fluster in the man's voice.

"Same as we do." Josh waved hello, which Braddon repeated with amusement as he greeted Jonah.

Jean stepped up, interpreting. "Jonah, this is an important friend of Dad's." Josh wondered if anyone else heard the tiny halt of new wonder in her voice before she used the title "Dad."

"We're going to take him and Mr. Palmer—" at which point Matt gave a nervous grin and waved hello as well "—fishing."

Jonah squinted up at Braddon and signed something.

"What'd he say?" Hal asked.

Jean gave a startled look to Josh, and then relayed, "Jonah asked if you were a big fish, too."

Josh choked down a laugh as he recognized the familiar sign. "It's a bit of a long story." He turned to Jonah. "Yes, he's a big fish." He grinned at Hal. "He's the biggest fish there is." *And I aim to land him.*

Braddon laughed. "That's a compliment, right?"

"Around here, it's a high compliment, Mr. Braddon," said Jean. "Come, let me show you around."

I was wrong, Josh thought to himself. *We're going to land him together.*

"I see you've been promoted yourself," Matt whispered as they walked down Aisle Avenue. "Congratulations, Dad."

Josh warmed with pride. That was a victory he could already claim as his, wasn't it? And today was the day to fight for that title. "Thanks. And thanks for getting Braddon here."

"You owe me. And I still think you're nuts. But I'm open to persuasion." He paused before adding, "She's still beautiful, by the way. But gutsier, and I suspect brainier than I remember. I can see your motivation. But I still think you're nuts."

"Maybe." Jean was beautiful. And gutsy. But *brainy* wasn't the right word for Jean. She was *wise*, which was a whole level above the kinds of brainy people he worked with every day. She was rare. She was a word he couldn't ever remember attributing to a woman before: she was *precious.*

I don't want to let her slip away a second time. Would it take hampering SymphoCync's future—and the colleagues he'd gathered there—to keep her? And Jonah?

Lord, I don't want this to be either/or. I want this to include everything. For a guilty moment, he wondered what Matt—or even Braddon—would think if they knew SymphoCync's CEO was *praying* right next to him. *He'd be as shocked to know it as I am to do it.* It was one of many changes he'd felt himself undergo since his first trip down Aisle Avenue.

The changes in him were startling, but good. As if he was peeling off an outer layer he'd somehow managed to acquire out in California, one that kept him stiff and numb. Now a different layer was coming out underneath—one that could breathe, that felt things more deeply and saw new details in the world he'd been too rushed to notice before. It struck him, as he took a deep breath to launch the sales pitch of a lifetime, that the shedding had already taken place. He couldn't—and wouldn't—put the old layer back on. He couldn't go back. Even if the cost became very high.

Would You really let it come to that? he asked the Father in Heaven, who seemed so much closer to him here than anywhere else. *Would You really ask that of me?*

They'd reached the inn. "Take a half hour or so to settle in, and then it's off to the creek, so bring your gear."

"You really *are* going to take me fishing," Braddon

scoffed and scratched his head, but with an amused expression.

"Humor me," Josh said. "I'm not a man to waste your time. I'm making a point here."

"And that point is?"

"In good time, Hal. In good time."

Braddon slanted a look at Matt. "Gutsy character, isn't he?"

Matt only nodded and opened the inn's front door for Braddon. Josh felt himself exhale as the pair walked in to where he knew Hailey would be waiting to see them to their rooms.

Jean looked at him. "You got him here. I can't believe you got him here."

He took Jean's hand. "Well, I figured if God's big enough to get me here, Hal Braddon shouldn't pose that much of a challenge." He'd shared his plan with Jean earlier. What he hadn't yet shared—because he didn't know it himself until just this moment—was that he would stay in Matrimony Valley no matter what today's outcome was.

The only question now was how much his staying would cost him and everyone who worked at SymphoCync.

"Well, listen to you," Jean marveled as she leaned in and kissed him gently on the cheek. The brush of her lips and the scent of her hair sent his pulse racing. He'd never really stopped loving her; he'd just let other things drown it out for a while. *Tell her.* As strong as the impulse roared to declare his resurging affections right there on Aisle Avenue, this wasn't the time. Once this whole business with Braddon was over, then that would be the time.

* * *

Jean could tell that while Hal Braddon was amused and intrigued by what he called "Josh's little field trip," Josh's second-in-command wasn't as enthused. In fact, the sandy-haired lanky man in round glasses and a black T-shirt looked rather lost in his fishing gear. "Hip waders," Matt Palmer said, looking down at the bulky boots-and-pants combination. "I'm wearing actual hip waders. That is what these things are called, isn't it?"

"Just 'waders,' I think. Although we have a few people who call them 'hippies,' if you prefer. With the creek water as cold as it is, you'll be glad for them no matter what they're called."

"Little man's got a pair of them, too, I see."

Jean turned to Jonah and signed, "Do you like the new waders Dad bought you?"

"Yep!" Jonah signed, nodding so vigorously that Jean felt no need to translate.

"So is Jonah going to be my fishing teacher?" Matt asked, nodding toward Jonah.

"You'll have to ask Jonah that." Jean turned to stand next to Matt, gesturing toward Jonah. She often had to coach people to talk directly to Jonah, allowing her to merely serve as translator rather than a messenger when people told her to "ask him this" or "ask him that."

It took Matt a second to realize the difference, but after a moment he bent down to Jonah's height and asked, "Are you my fishing teacher?" as Jean signed the words next to him.

"Daddy gets you, I get the big man," Jean voiced as Jonah signed. Braddon was, in fact, as imposing physically as he was financially. Both Josh and Matt were tall, but Hal Braddon had a good half foot on either of them—he had to be at least six foot four. A "big fish" indeed. It was a blessing that Jonah had no concept of what was at stake today. In his usual gregarious way, her son was simply excited to have new friends. He didn't share her anxiety that they'd be fishing with some of the most powerful men in the tech industry. Even the lieutenant governor hadn't made her so nervous, and they were planning his daughter's full wedding, not just an afternoon fishing trip.

Yes, well, her son's relationship with his father wasn't hanging in the balance of the lieutenant governor's wedding, was it?

Josh came across the street from where he'd been getting last-minute teaching tips from Bill. They'd both tried to convince Bill to come along on this little expedition. "Between you three, you got this more than covered," Bill insisted with a smile of confidence she didn't feel. Still, as Josh strolled across the street with the easy self-assurance that had gotten him this far, Jean began to hope. Her attempts at reserve, at holding her feelings in check and tamping down the desire to have Josh fully in their lives—not part-time, but full-time—were failing. The figure he cut in jeans and a simple shirt, waders thrown over one shoulder with a rod braced against the other, was 100 percent rugged handsome. How did he manage to be down-home and elegant at the same time like that? Only Josh Tyler could look so natural and still stand out like a beacon on a dark mountainside.

His gaze was ablaze with confidence as he caught her eye. "I will do this," it said, and she allowed herself to believe in him. The prospect of losing him a second time to the excesses of California was simply too much to bear.

When Jonah rushed up to meet Josh with a jubilant hug, Jean felt the last of her heart crack open. "Dad," Jonah signed, as if it was all the greeting required— and wasn't it? Hal Braddon had come out from the inn, but she didn't voice the silent exchange for the two men standing beside her. The lump in her throat made it impossible, and no one could miss the meaning.

"Son," Josh signed, hugging the boy. She saw his eyes close for just a moment. He was savoring the moment just as she was. *Let Braddon see what I see*, she prayed. *Let him see what we all see in this place and that man.*

Josh walked up to shake Braddon's hand. "You look like you were born to do this, Hal."

The man laughed. "I was just about to say the same thing about you. Not exactly my usual sphere of influence."

"Nah," said Josh as he turned the whole group toward the direction of the creek. "It's just like finance. You take a few minutes to master the cast, use the right bait, tug a little to set the deal and then reel 'em in."

Jean swallowed a laugh. Josh made the art of fly-fishing—something men enjoyed a lifetime of effort to master—sound easy. And maybe it was. If Jonah could catch a fish at age five, couldn't a middle-aged man of high intellect do the same in an afternoon? After all, he didn't need to catch a fish for this to work— although it helped. Braddon just needed to understand why Josh needed to be here. And Jonah was as much a part of that evidence as the natural beauty around them and the allure of the sport.

Chapter Twenty-One

"Ten and two and ten and two and…" Hal Braddon tipped his rod overhead back and forth before sending the line out over the creek in an impressive curl. "Ha! Will you look at that. Right where I planned to land it."

"A natural, just like I said," Josh complimented. "Don't wait for me to admit that you caught on faster than I did, because I won't."

"Well," said Braddon as he pulled in his line for another cast, "that boy of yours is a fine teacher. But I'm going to let you in on a little secret. I was born in Montana. We do a bit of fishing out there, you know."

Matt turned around from where he was standing a little downstream. "What?"

Josh pushed his hat back on his head. "You already knew how."

Braddon grinned. "I thought it was more fun if you didn't know. Besides, I wanted to see how you were going to play all this out." He leaned his pole against his shoulder. "So now you've set your hook. How about you reel this one in and tell me why I'm here."

Josh reeled in his line and stood next to Braddon. "I wanted you to see this, to see why I'm ready to sell you SymphoCync. But only on one condition."

Josh could practically hear Matt's gulp from the few yards downstream where he stood.

Josh walked over and stood next to Matt. "I'm promoting Matt to co-CEO. You can own the place, free and clear, but Matt and I will run it." He made a point of catching Jean's eye as she stood nearby on the riverbank. "I'll just be running my half mostly from here."

Jean's eyes went wide. He nodded slowly, meeting her startled stare, wanting to be sure she understood what he'd just declared. "I needed you to see why this place is just as important to me as SymphoCync. I'll sell you the company, but those are my terms. Matt's there, and he has as much authority as I do, but I'm here at least eighty percent of the time."

Braddon and Matt started talking both at once, but Josh didn't hear them. He just heard the splashes of Jean walking right into the water, shoes and all, and the exquisite sound of her breath as he took her into his arms and kissed her. At some point he was pretty sure his expensive pole fell into the water, but it didn't matter. Braddon could say yes or no to the deal, and it wouldn't change the decision he'd made. He'd arrange whatever setup it took to replant his life here, with Jean and with Jonah.

A splash of cold water droplets broke the kiss, and he pulled back to see Matt and Hal staring at him.

"What was I just saying about a flair for drama?" Braddon said, an amused look on his face. He turned to Matt. "What are we going to do with him?"

It was as close to a yes as Josh needed. He walked over and extended a hand to Hal while keeping the other hand firmly around Jean's. Yes, it made her wade a little farther into the water, but he doubted she minded at the moment.

"So it's a deal?" Josh asked, although it felt a bit more like he was gulping the words out.

"It's the most unusual deal I think I've ever done," Hal said, shaking Josh's hand. "But then again, I've always found you a most unusual man."

"I've always been the normal one," Matt joked, still looking a little shocked.

"Says who?" Josh teased. "Matt, the paperwork's all in that envelope I put on your hotel room desk this morning." He pulled Jean close. "Why don't you two head on back and go over it. I've got a few things to do here."

"I can just imagine. You know, I used to use 'going fishing' as an excuse to sneak away to a pretty girl, too. Mrs. Braddon ties a mean fly. You don't think I married her just for her good looks, do you?"

"I think I'm going to write in a 'no company fishing retreats' clause into that paperwork." Matt shook his head. "I can't understand what you both see in this. No offense, but it's boring."

"Peaceful," Josh and Hal both corrected at the same time.

"Get on over to that son of yours," Hal said, pointing to where Jonah sat playing with a truck on the bank a few feet away. "Tell him he's the best fly-fishing teacher I've ever had."

"I'll do that."

As he moved toward the bank, Hal stopped and turned. "Tyler, what would you have done if I said no?"

"Come here anyway."

Hal's grin returned. "Good call. The smart fisherman knows which fish are worth keeping, and which to let go for another day."

All four of them waded to the bank, where Hal and Matt gathered their gear and headed back to the inn and the awaiting paperwork. "Matt will be a great CEO," Josh said, meaning it. "I'd trust him with my life, even more so with my company. *Hal's* company," he corrected. "Wow, that's going to take some getting used to."

"You're sure?" Jean asked, a much larger question in her eyes.

In answer, Josh squatted down in front of Jonah and signed "How…say…" and then put his fingers together in the shape of a heart, nodding toward Jean.

Jonah crossed his forearms in front of his chest, then pointed at Josh.

"I love you," Josh said, repeating the sign and pointing to his son. "I love your mom, too," he said, making the same sign and pointing at her, adding the sign for "again." He looked deep into Jean's eyes, now brimming with tears, and simply said, "Still. I never stopped."

"Me, neither," she said, and then it became a tumble of arms and legs until Jonah popped up from the exuberant group hug and signed "family" with a huge smile on his face.

"Yep," Josh agreed with both hands and all his heart. "Family."

* * * * *

Dear Reader:

I love restoration stories. It warms my heart to read of wrongs put right, gaps closed, hurts healed and broken hearts mended. There's not enough of that in our world, is there? That's where the power of story wields its greatest strength—reminding us of what could be.

I love reinvention stories, too. Second chances, new purposes and discovered gifts all make a powerful difference to my heart. Josh, Jean, Jonah and the whole town of Matrimony Valley inspire me to remember how nothing is ever truly lost from God's view. Our Lord knows no lost causes—what better message could we hear?

I hope you'll come back to Matrimony Valley to watch Kelly Nelson, the straight-talking town florist and Lulu's devoted mother, get her own happy ending in the next Matrimony Valley series book coming soon.

Until then, remember that I'd love to hear from you at allic@alliepleiter.com, on social media (Instagram, Facebook and Twitter) and good old-fashioned mail at PO Box 7026, Villa Park, IL 60181.

Blessings,

COMING NEXT MONTH FROM
Love Inspired®

Available June 19, 2018

HIS NEW AMISH FAMILY
The Amish Bachelors • by Patricia Davids

Desperate to stop her *Englisch* cousin from selling the farm her uncle promised to her, widow Clara Fisher seeks the help of auctioneer Paul Bowman. Paul's always been a wandering spirit, but will sweet, stubborn Clara and her children suddenly fill his empty life with family and love?

HER FORGIVING AMISH HEART
Women of Lancaster County • by Rebecca Kertz

Leah Stoltzfus hasn't forgiven Henry Yoder for betraying her family years earlier. But Henry is a changed man. And when a family secret is unearthed, shaking Leah to her core, he's determined to support her. If only she could leave the past behind and open her heart to him...

THE SOLDIER'S REDEMPTION
Redemption Ranch • by Lee Tobin McClain

Finn Gallagher's drawn to his new rescue-dog caretaker, Kayla White, and her little boy. But the single mother's running from something in her past. And as he begins wishing the little family could be *his*, Finn must convince her to trust him with her secret.

FALLING FOR THE COWGIRL
Big Heart Ranch • by Tina Radcliffe

Hiring Amanda "AJ" McAlester as his assistant at the Big Heart Ranch isn't foreman Travis Maxwell's first choice—but his sisters insist she's perfect for the job. But with money on the line, AJ and her innovative ideas could put him at risk of losing everything...including his heart.

HIS TWO LITTLE BLESSINGS
Liberty Creek • by Mia Ross

When the school board threatens to cut her art program, Emma Calhoun plans to fight for the job she loves. And with banker Rick Marshall on board to help, she might just succeed. But will the handsome widower and his sweet little girls burrow their way into her heart?

THE COWBOY'S LITTLE GIRL
Bent Creek Blessings • by Kat Brookes

Cowboy Tucker Wade discovers he has a daughter he never knew about when his late wife's twin sister shows up on his doorstep. Now it's up to Autumn Myers to decide if he can be the kind of daddy her niece deserves.

LICNM0618

Get 4 FREE REWARDS!

We'll send you 2 FREE Books <u>plus</u> 2 FREE Mystery Gifts.

Love Inspired® books feature contemporary inspirational romances with Christian characters facing the challenges of life and love.

FREE
Value Over
$20

YES! Please send me 2 FREE Love Inspired® Romance novels and my 2 FREE mystery gifts (gifts are worth about $10 retail). After receiving them, if I don't wish to receive any more books, I can return the shipping statement marked "cancel." If I don't cancel, I will receive 6 brand-new novels every month and be billed just $5.24 for the regular-print edition or $5.74 each for the larger-print edition in the U.S., or $5.74 each for the regular-print edition or $6.24 each for the larger-print edition in Canada. That's a savings of at least 13% off the cover price. It's quite a bargain! Shipping and handling is just 50¢ per book in the U.S. and 75¢ per book in Canada*. I understand that accepting the 2 free books and gifts places me under no obligation to buy anything. I can always return a shipment and cancel at any time. The free books and gifts are mine to keep no matter what I decide.

Choose one: ☐ **Love Inspired® Romance**   ☐ **Love Inspired® Romance**
                 Regular-Print   **Larger-Print**
                 (105/305 IDN GMY4)   (122/322 IDN GMY4)

Name (please print)

Address   Apt. #

City   State/Province   Zip/Postal Code

> Mail to the **Reader Service:**
> **IN U.S.A.:** P.O. Box 1341, Buffalo, NY 14240-8531
> **IN CANADA:** P.O. Box 603, Fort Erie, Ontario L2A 5X3

Want to try two free books from another series? Call 1-800-873-8635 or visit www.ReaderService.com.

---

*Terms and prices subject to change without notice. Prices do not include applicable taxes. Sales tax applicable in N.Y. Canadian residents will be charged applicable taxes. Offer not valid in Quebec. This offer is limited to one order per household. Books received may not be as shown. Not valid for current subscribers to Love Inspired Romance books. All orders subject to approval. Credit or debit balances in a customer's account(s) may be offset by any other outstanding balance owed by or to the customer. Please allow 4 to 6 weeks for delivery. Offer available while quantities last.

Your Privacy—The Reader Service is committed to protecting your privacy. Our Privacy Policy is available online at www.ReaderService.com or upon request from the Reader Service. We make a portion of our mailing list available to reputable third parties that offer products we believe may interest you. If you prefer that we not exchange your name with third parties, or if you wish to clarify or modify your communication preferences, please visit us at www.ReaderService.com/consumerchoice or write to us at Reader Service Preference Service, P.O. Box 9062, Buffalo, NY 14240-9062. Include your complete name and address.

LII8

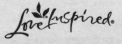